# You Can *Fool Me Once,* But *Never Twice*

**A Story Of Action, Suspense and
Romance That Follows Military Cops
From Africa To The US As It Takes Them
Twenty Years To Close The Case**

*Joseph Gillam*

iUniverse LLC
Bloomington

FOOL ME ONCE, NEVER TWICE
A STORY OF ACTION, SUSPENSE AND ROMANCE THAT
FOLLOWS MILITARY COPS FROM AFRICA TO THE US AS
IT TAKES THEM TWENTY YEARS TO CLOSE THE CASE

iUniverse books may be ordered through booksellers or by contacting:

iUniverse LLC
1663 Liberty Drive
Bloomington, IN 47403
www.iuniverse.com
1-800-Authors (1-800-288-4677)

ISBN: 978-1-4917-2635-8 (sc)
ISBN: 978-1-4917-2636-5 (e)

Printed in the United States of America.

iUniverse rev. date: 03/28/2014

# Dedication

Dedicated to all the fine Policewomen and Policemen that I served with around the world during my career. But, a particularly sharp salute to the 2300 Military Policemen that served with the Kagnew Station Military Police Company, Asmara, Eritrea during its African deployment from January 1956 to May 1973. As many of us that can meet each April in Myrtle Beach, SC for our reunion. I promise you that a good time is had by all.

# Acknowledgement

Bountiful thanks to my friend Geoffrey Pike who was my editor and sounding board through the process. Geoff found so many misspelled words I thought I was back in the fourth grade. Thanks Geoff.

# Introduction

Kagnew Station was a US Army installation in Asmara, Ethiopia. It had been an active installation from the early fifties until the mid-seventies. Before the formal activation of Kagnew Station, the American presence in Ethiopia had been a bit smaller. Radio Marina, as it was known in those days, tried to pass itself off as a radio relay station. This didn't fool too many people, and those that might have been fooled quickly saw the light when the great expanse of intercept antennas grew up in the 50s. It was called the antenna farm. The host command was the US Army Security Agency, which operated a rather large radio intercept station manned by some 4,000 soldiers. Asmara is situated on an 8,000-foot high mountain plateau, ideal for that mission. Other activities were a US Army Strategic Communication mission, a US Navy Communications Mission, a Deep Space Electronic Search Activity and an Air Force activity that managed and maintained flights that stopped on the Air Force around-the-world schedule.

Of course the post also had the full spectrum of housekeeping functions such as a club system, Post Exchange, Hospital, Commissary, Post Office and a big special services activity that assisted the community with their recreational fun. And naturally, to keep everybody on the up and up, there was a Military Police Company of about 75 policemen and their support personnel. The focus of our story, Military Policeman Joe Green, was stationed on Kagnew Station in the mid 60s.

For years soldiers had always said that an assignment to Korea was the best kept secret in the Army. None of those guys had ever been to Asmara. Just 90 miles up in the mountains from the Red Sea port of Massawa, it provided the best climate one could hope for. East Africa offered everything for the sportsman; hunting, fishing, water sports, and climbing and Americans were welcomed into the Italian sports leagues. The Art Deco architecture of Asmara's buildings built by Italians in the 1930s is still impressive today.

The local population included both the native Eritreans and a huge Italian population. The Italians were merchants, farmers and businessmen who had remained in the country from the Italian colonial days earlier in the century. The host nation welcomed the Italians, full well knowing that their skills were vital to the well-being of the province of Eritrea.

Everybody left Asmara with tears in their eyes and career soldiers fought tooth and nail to get back to Asmara. Friendships made in Asmara were more enduring than anywhere else in the Army. It was like Asmara cast a spell on you.

# Chapter 1

## The Assignment

It was a nice warm afternoon in Asmara. Not the stifling heat that was a usual August day. It was a nice day to ride around Asmara and the various Kagnew Station installations. I was working the afternoon shift this month on my usual activity of traffic enforcement and accident investigation. Not bad duty. No domestic disturbance calls, shoplifters or any of the other types of calls that no cop likes. I liked traffic. Most of it was self-initiated activities and each wreck brought a little something different to the table, no matter how minor might be the occurrence.

I had been on duty just about 2 hours when the radio called me a couple of minutes after 4:00 P.M. "Unit 28, this is Observer". Not the voice of the radio operator or even the Desk Sergeant, but that of Staff Sergeant Jack Fisher, the Patrol Supervisor. Sergeant Fisher was not the kind of leader that would snatch the radio from his subordinates. When he called you it meant business. What could it be? A major wreck? No, the radio operator would handle something like that. Not a paperwork error, I hadn't turned in anything yet. I had written two tickets and investigated one wreck where an Air Force Major's wife backed into an Army vehicle in the Post Office parking lot. Yep, that was it. I had not given her a ticket, but when I told her she would be responsible for the damage to the Army vehicle, she acted like I had singled her out.

She proceeded to tell me it was just an accident and that she had really not done anything wrong. I reminded her that the truck was properly parked and she had damaged it. I broke off the conversation as soon as possible, telling her to report the matter to her husband. Yea, it had to be her. I just hate complaints.

I answered, "Observer this is 28, just outside Track A Back Gate".

Sergeant Fisher's "Return To Station" cut through the car like a knife. I felt a serious chewing as I rogered the call and turned to drive across town to the MP Station.

Sergeant Fisher was what one would call an old soldier and a hard-core leader. He was a WWII and Korean War vet, a Military Policeman all the way. The story was that as a young MP he had written a speeding ticket to General Patton's driver as the General "caught fire" in the back of the car. It must be true because on the wall in his barrack's room was a framed letter from Patton that just simply thanked Fisher for his observance and dedication to duty. I did a good job for Sergeant Fisher and, as a Vietnam vet, I held a spot that nobody else on his squad had. I had never been on his bad side and was hoping that this was not the day.

I pulled up and parked in front of the MP Station and looked in the window. There was Sergeant Fisher looking through his blue tint glasses at me. He looked like he just could not wait for me to get inside. In I went and right off the top he asked what happened out there. I handed him my tickets and the accident report as I started the story about the Air Force wife. Nope, that was not it.

He said, "The Provost Marshal wants to see you ASAP. I don't know what it is, Green, but I hope it's not bad news".

He almost always called me Joe. A last name only showed some grit that was under his skin. "Go over to the Provost Marshal

Office and Master Sergeant Tucker will get you to the Provost Marshal. Then back here with the details."

The Provost Marshal Office was just a few blocks from the MP Station but there was enough time to reflect on the day. No, it was not the Major's wife. None of the tickets were out of the ordinary. Nothing bad that I could think of, so maybe it was good news. I parked behind the building and walked in the back door. My favorite door as it took me right past Giorgina's desk. We had been dating for awhile and I really felt strongly about our relationship. Bang, the light came on. I'll bet that was it. The Provost Marshal did not like me dating his secretary! Hum?

I went past her desk and we exchanged knowing smiles. Both the Provost Marshal and Master Sergeant Tucker knew full well we were dating, but we both kept it professional at work. I walked up to Sergeant Tucker's desk and we shook hands. We were co-workers and friends, too. I leaned over and asked if I was in hot water. He laughed and said, "Hell no, nothing of the kind, stop the sweating and report to the Colonel."

Lieutenant Colonel Nestler was a super true professional. The kind of officer that just knew everything. I truly respected him, and with Sergeant Tucker's news I was, all of the sudden, looking forward to the meeting. I knocked twice at his open door and he looked up with what one might call a smile. Field grade officers don't smile at enlisted men but he did show a warm face as he motioned me in his office.

I saluted and reported. He returned my salute and motioned to a chair and said to sit down. I turned to sit and only then did I notice Dutch Driggers sitting on the couch across the room. Mr. Driggers was another old hand. He was a CID Agent that carried the rank of Sergeant First Class. Dutch had been an MP for many years, then on to CID somewhere around his twenty-year anniversary. Now, my panic alarm began to sound again. What is he doing here?

Lieutenant Colonel Nestler called Sergeant Tucker into the room and Sergeant Tucker closed the door as he sat next to Mr. Driggers. Colonel Nestler began by saying that they needed some help from me. He gave a short thumbnail of a crime in the motor pool involving the theft of gas. Details were not specific and then he told me that the CID office was short. Mr. Driggers' partner was back at Fort Gordon at the MP School for some advanced training and the other of the two teams at Kagnew had gone up to the Sudan border to investigate a murder.

Colonel Nestler asked me if I would be willing to go to the CID Office for a couple of months and work with Mr. Driggers on this case. He explained that it would be almost all day work with the exception of maybe a few nights of surveillance. It would involve some close work with the Ethiopian police and maybe a bit of travel and TDY pay. He went on a bit with some minor details that I would go on separate rations and be exempt from any duties in the MP Company.

Heck, I had been ready after his first sentence and was hoping he would take a break so I could inject a yes. He finished his speech by telling me that with no shift work for a couple of months, it would free up a lot of time to chase his secretary around.

Everybody chuckled and that gave me my opening to accept the assignment. I threw in a thank you for having confidence in me and that I would do my very best for Mr. Driggers. I was tempted to make some comment about the secretary chasing but left it alone and kept things to the business at hand. I didn't have enough seniority in that room for trying to be funny. Colonel Nestler came up out of his chair, which was a military cue for everybody else to get on their feet. He gave me a small pat on the back and said that he knew I was the man for the job. With his hand still on my back, he guided me to the door. This was a signal that I did not have to salute or be formally dismissed. As we got to the door he stopped and said that he would now let us handle it. It was his way of passing the work down to where the rubber hit the road. He was a man of detail but not a micromanager.

Once outside, Sergeant Tucker told me to get with Dutch and get started as soon as possible. "Go back to the MP Station, turn your car and pistol in and tell Sergeant Fisher I'll call him about this."

He stopped at his desk and opened one of those big bottom Army desk drawers. He pulled out a brown paper sack and handed it to me saying, "You might need this. Keep it close and get it back to me when this gig is finished".

I looked in the bag and saw a snub-nosed .38, and a couple of boxes of ammunition along with a belt holster and a shoulder holster. I thanked him and we shook hands. Sergeant Tucker then said to come back to see him tomorrow and he would have the official documents for me to carry the pistol. Mr. Driggers and I then walked out the back door. I looked at Giorgina as I passed and smiled. She smiled back and flashed a big question mark with her face. I made a small "OK" sign and we were out the door.

Outside Mr. Driggers told me to get rid of the car and the MP Station's .45, then come up to see him. He then walked away in the direction of the CID Office. I got in the car and sat for a couple of minutes reflecting on the situation. I guess it was good deal. Militarily it was a chance to work at a higher level, always a good move. It should be interesting and maybe just a bit of excitement. Then too, like the Colonel said, it would free up some time for secretary chasing. Yes, all in all, I was happy.

I got back to the MP Station and found Sergeant Fisher. He was in the Patrol Supervisor's office and it was clear he was on the phone with Sergeant Tucker. "Oh, yes, Sergeant Tucker, I'm sure he can do it. Green is a good man. Wish I had ten of him. Just make sure he finds his way home when this assignment is finished."

Sergeant Fisher hung up the phone and stood up, "Good luck and good hunting. Dutch is a good man; pick his brain as much as you can. See you in a couple of months, but remember, call me if you need me." With that he gave me a pat on the back with a big squeeze and said, "Be careful; Sergeant Tucker gave me the headlines and there could be some ugly with this."

I walked out the back door of the MP Station and crossed the street to the CID office. Little did I know what a pivotal point this would be in my life.

# Chapter 2

## The Case

I walked from the MP Station to the CID Office. It was just a block away inside a fenced area that had at one time been a communications building. I walked in the front door and was met by Adrianna, an Italian woman of about 30 years of age. She was the office receptionist and secretary. She was a very pleasant lady who often stopped by the MP Station for a cup of coffee. I said hello, and she told me that she had heard I was coming to work with the Agents. News always travels fast in a police community, faster than a 100-watt Motorola radio can get it around. I smiled back at her and told her that now she would have company for her trips to the MP Station for coffee. She laughed and returned her nice smile.

I had been in the building several times before and knew where to find Mr. Driggers. I turned down the hall to the offices and was stopped by the CID Chief. Mr. Bob Barkus was a Chief Warrant 4 and had been at Kagnew Station for at least 7 years as the local gossip said. He was clearly the oldest person in the MP family. He looked to be just short of 60, but nobody was about to ask him, nor did anybody even have the nerve to check his driver's license in the files at the MP Desk. The word was that he had a "Rabbi" that had arranged for him to remain on active duty past 30 years and past the 55—year age mark for mandatory retirement.

"Rabbi" is an often-used Army term, someone of influence in the upper echelons that is your friend or maybe just indebted to you. Most "Rabbis" are full Colonels or above or some very senior Non-Commissioned Officers that have influence in high places.

He threw out his huge hand and I quickly acknowledged his handshake. He said, "Joe, glad to have you with us. Hope you will be happy here. Dutch will take good care of you, but my door is always open should you need anything." Then he squeezed my hand a bit harder, looked me right in the eyes and said, "Yes, anything at all, Joe."

His sincerity hit home and I really was beginning to feel at ease in this assignment.

I walked down the hall and came to Mr. Driggers' office. Not the corner office with the latest furniture. Metal army desk, older typewriter on a roller-typing table, standard issue metal file cabinet, and a couple of basic Army office chairs. I tapped on the doorframe of the open door and Mr. Driggers jumped up and said to come on in. He added that there would be no knocking, that this was our office. We small-talked a bit and he gave me a key to the gate and to the front door of the building. He told me that we would be sharing his office and that a desk would be delivered later tomorrow. We talked about work hours, meals, vehicles and other general housekeeping matters. He then told me to call him Dutch, that we would be partners for a couple of months and that we needed to become friends.

Then it was down to business. For the next hour he briefed me on the case. The annual IG inspection of the Transportation Motor Pool had noted that the fuel purchases and fuel consumption were far out of line over the past several years. The mission of the command had not grown nor had the vehicle fleet increased. Yet the fuel purchased had increased by 500 gallons a week. The IG had not included this in their written report to the command staff nor to the transportation officer but had informed the installation commander on a separate report. This was then sent this to CID through the Provost Marshal. Dutch went over the roster of personnel at the Transportation Office and the Motor Pool and said that they, about 35 of them, were our suspects.

He looked at his watch and so did I. It was after five o'clock. He stood up and said, "This place doesn't pay overtime; let's call it a day."

He told me to sleep on what we had discussed and that in the morning we would develop an investigative plan. I walked out with him and we parted company as he got into his private car. He drove an old Fiat with right-hand drive. The vehicle must have been twenty-five years old. The British had been the overseer of Ethiopia after the war and had initiated driving on the wrong side of the road. They were removed by UN mandate in 1957 but the country continued to drive on the right until the early 60s.

I walked down to the MP Station parking lot and got into my newer Fiat. I noted that I had just enough time to get to the barracks, change into civvies and get to Giorgina's house at a decent hour. She lived with her mother and father and it was understood that gentleman callers did not arrive after 7 o'clock. Old school customs. It would be nice to discuss the day's activities with Giorgina. I'm sure her job had made her aware of the theft, but she had been professional enough not to mention it to me. It would be nice to talk shop with her.

# Chapter 3

## *Giorgina*

I had met Giorgina on day two in Asmara. I was in-processing and had made a call on the Provost Marshal Office to meet the Operations Sergeant, Master Sergeant Tucker. I had arrived about 8:30 A.M. and found that both Sergeant Tucker and the Provost Marshal were out on some matter leaving only Giorgina in the office. Giorgina was a strikingly beautiful girl. Just my age I guessed, 25 or 26 years old. She was petite at about 5'03" or so and very well-proportioned with a beautiful Mediterranean complexion with big brown eyes. I took in all of her, stopping at her left hand. No ring! What was wrong with the male population in this area?

I introduced myself and told her of the purpose of my visit. She explained that the Provost Marshal and the Sergeant had gone to the pistol range to see the MPs shooting and that they were due back about 9:30 A.M. or so. She offered me a cup of coffee and a seat next to her desk. We talked for a bit as she fumbled around with filing or some such task. I slowly steered the conversation to the social happening in the community and she acknowledged that she spent most of her time at home and did not go out too often. What an opportunity! Was that a casual comment or was she giving me an opening? Well, I took it and just as the Provost

Marshal walked in we sealed a deal for dinner that night in downtown Asmara.

I snapped to attention and introduced myself to Lieutenant Colonel Nestler and his sergeant, Master Sergeant Tucker. Colonel Nestler gave me a textbook "welcome aboard" and "I'm sure you will enjoy it here" as he dashed into his office. Sergeant Tucker got himself a cup of coffee, and asked me about my past assignments, my military goals and myself. Good soldier-of-the-month board questions that every soldier should be able to answer in an impressive way. He then asked me to be his guest at the club for dinner. He did not mention when, but when I accepted, he asked how tomorrow night would work for me. I said great and he said to meet him in the club bar about 7:00 P.M. and we would have a drink before dinner.

What a break! Had he said tonight I don't know what I would have done. None of the three choices were worth a hoot. Break the date with Giorgina, which was by far the worst choice? Stymie around with Sergeant Tucker that I had prior plans? He might have interpreted that in a wrong way. Show up with his secretary? Might not have been a good idea. But, after 24 hours in Asmara, my social calendar was filling up nicely.

I thanked Sergeant Tucker and headed for the door. I gave Giorgina the biggest smile I had and said good-bye as I walked past her desk. I walked around post the rest of the day and finished my in-processing. Last stop was the central issue point where I picked up a load of MP equipment; leather gear, arm brassards, patches and the extra uniforms that are standard MP issue. I walked back to the MP Company with two armloads of stuff and had to do a juggling act a couple of times to salute passing officers. I was met at the door of the MP Company by one of the houseboys, Haile. He took possession of the uniforms and equipment and said he would have them ready in the morning. Nothing left to do but get ready for my date.

Giorgina had said that her house was well off the main streets so she had suggested we meet at the restaurant. Once dressed, I walked to the main gate and looked for a cab. When I did not see one, I asked the MP on duty there how to catch a cab. He pointed to a line of horse carts and said they will take you to anyplace in Asmara. He referred to them as "gerry carts". I jumped into the first one in line and handed the driver the address Giorgina had given me. He looked at it and jerked the horse cart out into traffic. Off we went at a smooth trot. He said it was about 10 minutes away, so I sat back and enjoyed the ride.

I arrived at the restaurant about 20 minutes before the scheduled time. I surveyed the scene and what did I see? There was Giorgina standing at the door. She was even more pleasing on the eyes now than when she had been at work. She had changed clothes and was wearing an outfit that did just a little bit more to show her good looks. I walked up and told her I was sorry I was late. She grabbed my arm, smiled and said not to let that happen again.

We had a great dinner of pasta with meat sauce, salad and a couple of glasses of wine. No dessert, but some espresso coffee at the bar after dinner. It was now a bit after ten and she said that she had to be at work in the morning and it was time to go. We walked outside and I saw a little yellow cab parked just up the street. I took her arm and we walked to the ca,d . As we walked along she dropped her hand into mine and gave it a squeeze as she thanked me for a great evening. She got into the cab and I got in next to her. She told me that she lived with her parents and they were not big on company late at night. OK, I told her. I just wanted to see her safely home. She held my arm as the cab drove the 5 minutes through back streets and traffic circles. We arrived at a one-story stone home surrounded by a stone fence. Giorgina leaned over and gave me a tiny hug and again thanked me for dinner. Then she was out of the cab, through the gate and into the darkness of her yard almost like a dream. I told the driver "Kagnew Station" and away he went. I reflected on a wonderful evening with a great girl as I rode back to post.

For the next year Giorgina and I saw each other as often as we could. Every night when I was on the day shift. An early dinner when I was on the mid-shift. And when I was on the afternoon shift, I would stop by her house in the early evening while on patrol to spend a couple of minutes with her. Of course we had my days off to also be together. Now remember this was the 60's and boy-girl relationships were not what they were a few years later or as they are today. As things progressed along, I asked her to go to Massawa with me for a weekend. I suggested camping on the beach. She smiled and said that would be great. We talked and planned and made a packing list. I was looking forward to this trip and thinking that it might bring us to a new plateau. I picked her up bright and early on a Saturday morning and was slightly set back to see her younger brother, Alberto, walking right to the car with us carrying his weekend bag. She saw the look on my face and said that her mother was sending Alberto along.

Now don't get me wrong, Alberto was a nice kid, about 19 years old, but it was clear his mother had given him some strong marching orders. Oh, well, we had a nice weekend. We ate at some nice seafood restaurants, went walking through old Italian sections of Massawa and enjoyed our camping on the beach. I had brought two big Army sleeping bags. When we got ready to settle down for the night, Alberto grabbed one, jumped in and zipped up. It had been a big day for him and he was asleep in a flash. Giorgina came back from the beach bathrooms in pajamas and got into the second sleeping bag. I saw myself sleeping on the sand wrapped in an old Army blanket I had in my car. I guess I had that "oh hum" look on my face. Giorgina smiled as she threw the unzipped sleeping bag open and waved me in. I didn't need a second invitation. In I got and zipped up. I guess it had been a big day for her, too, for she gave me a warm hug and was immediately off to sleep. It took me a bit to get to sleep, but I thought what a lucky guy I was as I drifted off to sleep.

# Chapter 4

## The Investigative Plan

After the first meeting with Dutch in the CID Office, I had dashed downtown to see Giorgina. Sergeant Tucker had told her of my new assignment, and in fact she seemed to know more about it than me. We brought each other up to speed over a plate of pasta her mother had made for dinner. Giorgina filled in a couple of things Dutch had not mentioned. She had read the IG Report before filing it and had typed the correspondence from the Provost Marshal to the Installation Commander. She was in the process of telling me she was sorry she had not told me about this major matter sooner when I stopped her. It was her professionalism that kept matters on a need-to-know basis. I respected her for that trait.

I left her house a bit earlier than usual. I wanted to go back to my room to brush up on some police techniques to include the procedures for the formulation of an investigative plan. Once back at my room I dug out my box of police textbooks. Over the years, since MP School, I had taken several college courses on police subjects and had accumulated a small library. I spent a couple of hours reading, and then I drifted off to sleep with thoughts of the case.

Next morning I was up before daylight. I showered and shaved and selected an outfit of civilian clothes that would be in sync with what I had seen the agents wearing. I unlocked my locker and got the .38 out. Then locked it back up. I didn't yet have the credentials that Sergeant Tucker had said to pick up from him and I did not want to appear too gung-ho in the eyes of Dutch and Mr. Barkus.

I got my Fiat from the parking lot and headed to the CID Office. It looked dark, so I walked to the MP Station for some coffee. The day shift was just going on the road and I was stopped a half dozen times with questions. Everybody knew I was on some temporary CID assignment and wanted to know what was up. I reminded them of the two agents out on the murder on the Sudan border and that Dutch's partner was back at Fort Gordon for training. I told them that I had been detailed to help Dutch with some of his work until those guys got back in town. Every time I told it I got it better and all responded with a positive nod.

I got my coffee and was standing outside the back of the MP Station when I saw Dutch round the corner in his ancient right-hand drive Fiat. I gulped down a couple of sips so I could walk fast without spilling and headed to the CID Office. I met Dutch at the front door just as he was taking his key out of the lock. Quicker than a bushbuck he took the coffee from me, smiled and said that he knew I would be a good partner. After that I always showed up with two cups of coffee.

We spent a couple of hours reviewing the case and developing our investigative plan. Dutch reminded me that investigative work was not the adrenalin rush of road patrol. You work on a case for weeks, sometimes months, and don't get the thrill until the big arrest at the end of your work. But, Dutch said, that the thrill at the end of a big case was equal to a months-worth of road patrol satisfactions.

Our plan was to concentrate on the three people that could be driving the train in this theft: Captain James Watson, the Transportation Officer; First Lieutenant William Falks, the Motor Pool Officer in Charge and Sergeant First Class Anthony Lucas, the Non—Commissioned Officer in Charge. We would first do background and financial checks on these three and see what popped up. Then it would be into the paperwork of the gasoline deliveries. We would also identify the delivery company and its drivers as well as their procedures. Someplace along the way we should find a bunch of money and a lot of gallons of gasoline.

I was beginning to see what all cops talked about: investigative work was a lot of legwork and paperwork.

# Chapter 5

## Starting Down The Trail

The first thing Dutch wanted to do was a background check on our three main players. He picked up the telephone and made a call to the Non-Commissioned Officer in Charge of Military Personnel. I listened as he talked. He told the Sergeant that he was sending his partner down to pick up three personnel files. He identified the men and told the Sergeant that Investigator Green would be there within the hour. He tapped me on the shoulder like I was a bench player about to go into the game and pointed towards the door. I jumped up like I was that player and was out the door when Dutch called me back. "Don't forget to show your credentials and properly identify yourself." Yep I said and told him that I would stop by and see Sergeant Tucker on the way. Dutch smiled and gave me a mock salute and tossed me the keys to his unmarked CID sedan.

I stopped at the Provost Marshal Office and went in the back door that would take me past Giorgina's desk. We exchanged smiles as I approached Sergeant Tucker's desk. That smile was like 10 gallons of gasoline. It filled my tank and would make me run smooth for the rest of the day.

Sergeant Tucker reached into his top desk drawer and handed me a nice looking leather wallet-sized folder. I opened it and looked at my picture on a very nice set of "Provost Marshal Investigator" credentials and a DA Form 2818, authority to carry concealed weapons. A step up from all those uniformed MPs riding around in those 75,000-mile sedans.

I thanked him and was about to leave when I heard the voice of Lieutenant Colonel Nestler. "Hold on there, Investigator, you got some mail here." He walked out of his office and handed me an envelope with just my hand-written last name in the address field. I opened it and saw it was a check in the amount of $212.00 from the US Treasury to me. He said, "That's your civilian clothing allowance. Dutch will tell you what you might need."

In the 60s that was a nice sum of money. I figured that it would buy me some nice clothes and a little left over for a first-class dinner with Giorgina in a top downtown spot. I headed out the back door and flashed Giorgina a nice big smile, which she returned.

I drove to military personnel where I introduced myself to the Non-Commissioned Officer in Charge, who handed me a rather large envelope. He asked how Dutch was doing, saying he had not seen him in a couple of months. I looked at his chest. Staff Sergeant Allen sported some nice ribbons including a silver star and a couple of purple hearts. He said that he and Dutch had been in the same MP Company during the Korean War. Sergeant Allen went on to tell me how they had both got shot up when a squad of Chinese Communists attacked their road checkpoint one night. His wounds caused him to be reclassified from the MPs to Personnel. He told me that anytime we needed something, he would have it ASAP and on the QT. A nice guy to know, I thanked him and gave him a firm handshake as I departed.

I took the envelope back to the office and noted that there was a second desk in Dutch's office. Nothing fancy—a standard issued gray metal Army desk with a matching chair that was brand new.

I looked over at Dutch's chair, which was well worn and had clearly seen better days. I started to roll the new chair to Dutch's desk and he stopped me. "No, my butt fits just right in this one. Got a nice spot in the stuffing removed for my 'roids." We both laughed as Dutch opened the envelope and pulled out the three military 201 personnel files.

We spent the rest of the morning going through those files. Some interesting facts were uncovered. All three men were from Georgia and did not live but 25 miles apart. Captain Watson had been a Lieutenant Colonel in the Korean War but rifted back after the war. Lieutenant Flaks was on thin ice. He had several poor evaluations and had been passed over for promotion. Once he got to Asmara and went to work of Captain Watson, his evaluations were excellent. Sergeant Lucas had worked for Captain Watson at a past assignment at Fort Sill, OK, where his evaluations were glowing. He then went to Germany where he received mediocre report cards and had some disciplinary action from a bar fight in Frankfurt. Then on to Asmara where his evaluations from Lieutenant Falks were again excellent. It was clear that this trio was tighter than the three musketeers!

While I caught up typing the reading file in the casebook, Dutch drafted an undeveloped lead message back to CID Headquarters in Falls Church, VA, asking for a financial report on these three. We then worked together as Dutch walked me through how to write a letter for the Installation Commander's signature that would give us access to their bank records at the Kagnew Station Credit Union. Dutch ran the drafts past Mr. Barkus who approved them and we took both documents to Adriana who said she would have them done by the close of business. Dutch told her that would be great but he would be gone the rest of the day and would 9:30 A.M. tomorrow morning be OK with her. That was his way of not wanting to put a stress on Adriana. I learned that Dutch never put himself first. But in later years I would see one time when he did put himself first.

Then Dutch said, "Let's go for a ride. You still got the car keys?"

We walked outside and he got into the passenger seat, which was my sign to drive. I started up the Dodge and asked him where we were going.

"No place particular, I just think it best to be out of the office." He leaned over, looked at the gas gage, which was bouncing off of one—quarter. "Let's go to the motor pool and see if they have any gas left."

We both laughed as I drove to the Motor Pool. The Dodge was an Army car, ordered on the same contracts with the olive drab vehicles, but just painted light blue instead of green. At maybe Fort Hood or Fort Lewis, it might not have been noticed but at Kagnew Station one might just as well have painted CID on the doors in two-foot letters. Dutch told me that when they needed a covert car, they would get a rental from downtown.

We gassed up and took a few extra seconds sizing up the lay of the land in the Motor Pool. We had both been there hundreds of times before but we now looked at it in a different way. All of the sudden it was not our gas and repair point, it was a felony crime scene.

Dutch looked over at me as I was studying the gas pumps, the gasoline delivery area and the offices. He said, "Funny how cops see thing differently. It's like riding up to a gas station; a cop always looks inside for the all-clear, insuring they are not getting robbed. A civilian just ambles in with money in his hand." I would remember those words. We rode around for about an hour, looking out the windows and listening to the police radio. There was nothing going on, a quiet day in Africa.

Dutch looked at his watch and again repeated his favorite saying, "This place don't pay overtime, head to the house," house being police jargon for the station, office, or wherever one worked.

As we drove back, I asked Dutch what he had going on for dinner. He had nothing planned so I asked him if he would go out with Giorgina and me to our favorite little spaghetti spot downtown. He was hesitant, but with a little arm-twisting I got him to agree. He said that he would have to go stag in that he had not met any ladies yet in Asmara. I had been in Asmara for over a year and Dutch was there when I arrived. I was beginning to learn just what a loner he was. He said he would meet us there, so I gave him the address as we parked the CID sedan and headed to our private cars.

# Chapter 6

## *Getting To Know Dutch*

I picked up Giorgina and we drove to our favorite side street restaurant to meet Dutch. Gindae St was wide enough for parking on both sides. The restaurant was just a couple of doors down from Queen Elizabeth St. Funny, the British had never been very popular as the overseers of Ethiopia but years after their departure the main street in Asmara still carried the name of Queen Elizabeth. Just as we were getting out of my car, I saw Dutch pull up in his classic Fiat. It was a prewar model but he kept it running like new. I guess I would have trusted it to go anyplace. Dutch had taken it down the mountain several times to Massawa. He said his only problem was that he had to stop at the Half Way House and reset the carburetor for the changes in altitude. That was a common practice for the older cars and Jessie Dobbins, the retired G.I. who owned the Half Way House restaurant and hotel, employed a mechanic for a little side money.

We walked in and the waiter recognized us and gave us a nice table by the window. I had invited Dutch but before I could say a thing, he had ordered a nice bottle of Italian Chianti wine. I noted that Dutch ordered in Italian and also had a short conversation with the waiter. I had not known of Dutch's language ability. I was doing my best to learn Italian and making some progress, but Dutch left me in his dust. To make matters worse Giorgina picked up on his skill and the talk changed to Italian. I could barely keep up with the conversation, understanding about 90 percent but my speaking skills were far below my comprehending ability. The waiter opened the wine and poured each of us a glass. We talked a bit and I asked Dutch where he learned his Italian. Dutch then told us about his service in the Second World War. He had been stationed in Italy with the occupation forces after the war. He told us of his wartime assignments in England, through France and into Germany, before his MP Company was sent to Italy. He said he had no close family so elected to stay in Italy after the war. He told us how that was where his interest in investigations was seeded when he was detailed to conduct black market investigations. We talked for over an hour as Dutch told some very interesting stories. He then told us of his assignments in the states, the Korean War, back to Germany, back to the states to CID school, back to Italy, and then on to Africa. As we talked it didn't take me long to cover my short six years in the Army. Dutch asked about Vietnam. He said that he guessed that he would make it to Vietnam, but was not in a hurry. After World War II and the Korean War, he was not interested in another war. That might be pushing his luck. Giorgina then talked about what it was like being Italian in Africa. She had been born in Italy and spent most of her early life there. Her father retired from the Italian army and the family moved to Eritrea to be close to some relatives. She felt very lucky to have gotten a job on the American installation. She had first been a low-grade typist in the headquarters building; then shortly after that she had interviewed and moved up to her job with the Provost Marshal. She said that she found it interesting and was able to feel the excitement as she read the police reports and blotters.

All the talk was shop; nobody talked anything about family or personal matters. I guess that was normal. Dutch in his forties would not of had a lot in common with Giorgina and me in our twenties. But I did get a renewed understanding of Dutch. He spoke softly and it was evident through his conversation that he was a gentle man who clearly cared for others. These are not traits displayed by all police officers.

The specialty of the house, ravioli, arrived and it got quiet as we ate. We finished our dinner and, as was the custom, moved to the bar for espresso coffee. It was a bit after 10:00 P.M. and tomorrow was a workday for all. I knew that Giorgina rode the bus which was not the fastest way to get around Asmara. I told her to take my car and I asked Dutch if I could ride with him. I called the waiter for the check but Dutch had already taken care of it, to include the tip.

We walked outside and I gave Giorgina the keys to my car. She thanked me, gave me a nice hug, thanked Dutch and headed home. Dutch and I got into his car and started back to Kagnew Station. He told me I was very lucky to have Giorgina. I agreed and asked him if he was seeing someone. He said that he had dated a couple of women, but there was not a large selection in his age group. I thought about that; yes, very few American women that were not married. Maybe a schoolteacher or two but not too many, and almost all the Italian women were married. Yes, slim pickings for somebody in their forties.

As a CID Agent, Dutch qualified for a room in the bachelor officers' quarters. He dropped me at the MP Company on his way home. We talked a couple of minutes; I thanked him again for the evening and watched as his Fiat drove up the street. I had a new appreciation for Dutch and hoped to be able to call him a friend. He was a special guy.

# Chapter 7

# Leg Work and Paper Work

Dutch and I spent the next couple of weeks digging out all we could find about the gasoline utilization and deliveries to the Motor Pool. We did not go directly to the Motor Pool, but got our information from other sources. The IG report contained fuel purchases and consumption for the past five years. The installation S-4 Office had records of vehicle acquirements and retirements with their yearly mileages. The command had some 450 military vehicles. We did a calculation on each vehicle figuring its consumption. All in all it appeared that starting about a year and a half ago the monthly purchases of gasoline from the local national distributor had risen over 2,000 gallons a month without any justification. We had a felony theft.

We reviewed the accounts of the three musketeers at the only US banking facility in Africa, The Kagnew Station Credit Union. Each had an account and nothing too much out of line with the exception of Sergeant Lucas. Shortly after his arrival in Asmara about two years ago, he had borrowed money for a new car and furniture for his off—post rental house. He had been set up on monthly payments for the next thirty months. He made the payments right on time; then all of the sudden, started dumping money on the loan and had it paid off in less than a year. Clearly he had come into some money.

There was a strong probability that the local national company that supplied the fuel was involved in some way. This necessitated going to the Ethiopian Police and initiating a joint investigation. We could have done some basic snooping and maybe developed some leads. But at some point the local police would be needed to make a case against any local nationals involved. Then too, the Status of Forces Agreement mandated that all off-post police activities be jointly coordinated.

Bright and early on a Monday morning Dutch and I headed to the Asmara Police Station to meet with Ethiopian detectives. The CID Office employed a local national, Zehai, who carried the job title of investigator/translator. Zehai went with us to the Asmara Police Station.

Every other Saturday afternoon Mr. Barkus had a shrimp boil in the patio in the backyard of the CID Office. Two guys would go to Massawa early in the morning, buy the shrimp, and then drive back up the mountain, arriving not later than 12:30 pm. As the lowest ranking person in the CID office, I was quickly assigned to go to Massawa with Zehai every other week. When we got back, the fire would be burning, the water seasoned and boiling and the 100 or so pounds of shrimp would be dumped into the huge pot of water. Zehai and I would head out around 5:30 A.M. or so. We quickly established the pattern that he would drive down to Massawa and I would drive back up the mountain, or as it was sometimes called, "the hill". The road was about 127 kilometers from Asmara to Massawa. Remember in that distance you traveled from 8,000 ft elevation to sea level. The first half of the trip was down the mountain with switchback curves and steep grades, often of 8 to 10%. Then the Halfway House and across the desert or flats, as it was called, to Massawa. In three years I just don't know how many trips I made up and down the hill. I always loved it. The Italians called Asmara "the city in the clouds." When you made the last curve out of Asmara heading down, you had a long view of the road winding down the mountain. Many times you would see clouds below you as you looked across the expanse to the Red Sea far in the distance.

Adriana provided the sauce and Mr. Barkus provided the beer as well as the shrimp, all out of his pocket. In the 1960s the Army worked a five and a half day workweek. This made a nice way to finish the week. All from the Provost Marshal Office, MP Company, MP Station and, of course the CID office were invited. The average turnout was 60 or so folks.

The CID Office was a good place to eat. Several times a month Adriana would whip up some excellent pasta with her home-made sauce. There was an ancient gas grill behind the office and she would head out there mid-morning and start lunch. For something special she would make it for dinner. The map room in the office was nice and big and had a large flat table. Over the years the Agents had collected up some dishes, wine glasses and silverware. The table could be set to look real nice. Along the back fence Dutch kept a garden. He had a nice selection of herbs, lettuces, tomatoes and onions. Dutch could be seen at his garden on weekends and sometimes the lunch hour if he was not going to lunch or working. It was his chief off-duty activity, along with his ancient Fiat.

Dutch, Zehai and I arrived at the Main Asmara Police Station and made our way to the detectives on the third floor. Do not compare this office with NYPD or some such. This was Africa in the 1960s. Four detectives manned the entire detective office. They shared one telephone and one very old typewriter and worked in a large common office. If you had your car broken into or something stolen from your house or yard, you were on your own. No follow-up in those kinds of cases. These guys went to work on cases where the government was the victim and some major cases. They were kind of obligated to help us by the Status of Forces Agreement, but that did not mean they always did. They were spread thin with no help on the horizon or in the pipeline.

Most, if not all, of the lead people in the government were Ethiopian, not Eritrean from our local province in the country. Eritrea had been a separate country before the Second World War but became part of the British protectorate after the war. When the British withdrew in the 50s, Haile Selassie continued to oversee Eritrea and formally annexed it in 1962. Eritreans did not like this so they were not trusted in positions of authority. There were exceptions and Sergeant Adonay Bereket was one of them. Not only was he Eritrean, but also Jewish. He was assigned to work with us on the case. His command of English was excellent as was his Italian and several of the 40 some languages spoken in his country. He would come to be my point-of—contact on this case as well as future dealings with the Asmara police. He would also come to be a good friend.

We sat at a rather large flat worktable in the detective office and for over an hour or so explained the case to Adonay. From time to time his boss would stop by the table and listen in on the talk. When he screwed his face due to lack of understanding, Zehai gave him some translation. The case seemed to interest him. Yes, the American installation was the victim, but so was the Ethiopian government. A lot of tax dollars were not being paid as this gasoline made its way onto the black market. It looked like we could count on them for a lot of help.

Dutch finished his briefing and Adonay smiled, "Looks like a good deal for us. You guys have done a ton of work and we will reap the benefits of seizure and taxes."

Dutch quickly came back, "No sir, looks like a good deal for us. You will do a bunch of work and we will arrest the three criminals."

Everybody laughed and the Ethiopian Captain said that it was time for coffee. We all walked across the street to a coffee bar agreeing that Zehai and Adonay would continue the "off post" investigation while Dutch and I continued our efforts. An easy and friendly meeting, it was my first lesson in learning that the Ethiopian people are very friendly and accommodating.

# Chapter 8

## *The Tree is Growing Fruit*

We had been working on this case for over a month. The first couple of weeks were kind of slow, as we had to pick up a couple of other cases until Tim Wallace and Larry Higgins got back from their murder investigation on the Sudan border. Mr. Barkus had even picked up a couple of cases. I would learn later that as the Chief it was not his style to work cases. An AWOL GI had stolen a motor pool jeep and driven to Massawa, then on up the coast to the border of Sudan. He was not allowed to cross the border so he spent some time in the little border town until he ran out of money. Broke, he tried to break into a store one night and the merchant who lived upstairs came down to see what was causing the noise. The GI struggled with the merchant who got stabbed and killed in the fight. Wallace and Higgins managed only a "cover investigation" to the Ethiopian police investigation. The host nation decided to exercise jurisdiction and tried and hung the soldier. Hanging was the method in capital cases. Two local national employees of the Army hospital went down later to retrieve his remains for shipment to his family in the states.

Tim and Larry were old friends. They had been partners in Asmara for a couple of years. Before that they had both been stationed at Fort Carson where they were also partners. They got along great. One look at a case and they knew exactly what each would do and moved in quickly. Their style was fast and gruff, not the methodical ways of Dutch. I was glad I was learning from Dutch.

The undeveloped lead we had sent to CID Headquarters came back. It was very fruitful. Special Agents from the Fort Stewart, Georgia, CID Office had gone to the area where the three suspects lived and learned that each had a nice bank account that had begun growing about 18 months ago. The regular deposits were cash deposited by various family members of the suspects. Now it is not unusual for soldiers, officers or enlisted, to send money home. The general lower cost of living in an assignment like Africa allowed and even encouraged saving. So this was not damming evidence in itself, but it did go on our side of the scales. They returned the lead with their report of investigation. We sent a message back asking that the family not be interviewed just yet so as not to alert the suspects. We felt very close to an apprehension and did not want to alert our suspects.

Now remember Kagnew Station was a small post and filled with "homesteaders", an Army buzzword for soldiers that extend their assignment. In those days it was not uncommon to meet people that had been stationed there for 6 to 8 years straight. Master Sergeant Lindquist, the Non-commissioned Officer in charge of special services, even owned his own home in Asmara. He extended until the 10-year time limit on being outside of the United States, left his family in Asmara, took a short tour in Korea and then had his "Rabbi" work him back to Asmara. With all these politics in place we could not be sure that the three suspects had not been alerted to our investigation. But one thing nice about conducting an investigation at Kagnew Station: nobody was a flight risk! In those days travel into the country was on a red passport and upon arrival the passports were collected by the command and held until your departure.

Dutch and I had gone downtown for lunch at a little spot that was his favorite. Just as good as mine, but it was in the off-limits area of Asmara known as the Bosh. MPs were famous for frequenting spots in the Bosh. There was no competition from other soldiers and the GI inflation rate had not set in yet. It was not my first trip to the Bosh.

We had a small plate of pasta and then split a fruit bowl. No wine, as we were still on duty, but we did each have a bottle of nice, cold sparkling mineral water. We got back in Dutch's blue Dodge to head to post and as soon as we turned on the radio we had a call, "CID-72, go to Central Police Station and meet Investigator Zehai." Dutch rogered the call and I headed to the Ethiopian Police Station. Not like Zehai to be directing Dutch around. His protocol was to write an investigative summary for the casebook and report in person. We both agreed that Zehai and Adonay must have either hit a big snag or come up with something good.

We parked and climbed the stairs to the Detective's Office on the third floor of the police building. There was Zehai and Adonay with several boxes of papers. They were going through them at a quick pace and pulling one set out every 10 or 12 sets of papers. The papers were several different forms and hand-written slips stapled together. They were in Tigrinya so Dutch and I were in the dark. Adonay began to tell us of their venture to the gasoline distributor. They learned that only one driver, an Eritrean, delivered the gasoline to Kagnew Station. The weekly order had been increased from 1500 gallons to 2000 gallons about 18 months ago. The delivery tickets affixed to the paperwork were the end-of-day accounting for the tank trailer. In other words the driver went to the tank farm in the morning and filled his trailer with 2000 gallons of fuel. He then delivered 500 gallons someplace and the truck would print a ticket for that delivery. Then on to Kagnew Station and drop 1500 gallons, and the truck would print that ticket. Then to account for his load the driver would key in the end-of-day status and it would print a 2000-gallon ticket. He was then getting that signed by and affixing it to his paperwork with the 2000-gallon order. If you were not familiar with the various forms printed by the truck, you would be none the wiser. Zehai said this was further complicated by the fact that the delivery company had several different models of trucks and each had a different format for delivery receipts.

They had questioned the driver who was scared to death. No local national wanted to go through the Ethiopian court system. There was no such thing as plea-bargaining, reduced sentences or first offender status. All sentences were harsh and if the government was the victim of a crime, they were particularly harsh. In addition to confinement, most sentences would include lashes. The driver had made a full confession and would be a credible witness against the Americans in a court-martial.

We were ready to make the arrests. We wanted to insure that all bases were covered in both military law and that of the host nation. We set a meeting for 9:00 A.M. in the morning at the CID Office. We would have there the Ethiopian police, their legal representative, the CID folks and a lawyer from the Post Staff Judge Advocate Office.

After the meeting concluded, we shook hands around the room and the Detective Captain moved us all across the street to seal the deal with coffee. After a couple of rounds of espresso, and I'm not sure but there might have been a touch of cognac in the coffee, Dutch, Zehai and I headed back to the office.

On the way back Dutch looked at his watch and uttered his favorite line, "You know, Joe, this place don't pay overtime."

I smiled and acknowledged his statement. Then Dutch added, "But tonight I guess we will just have to work off the clock. We need to go over this and make sure we have not missed something."

That was an investigative trait I learned from Dutch. He was most meticulous, never missing the smallest of details. Fine with me, I was looking forward as to how this case would close. We walked in the office just a few minutes before five. I called Giorgina at the Provost Marshal Office and told her I would not be by tonight, as we had to work late. She said to be careful and sounded relieved when I told her that it might be a paper cut at worst, that we were getting ready to close the case, and that we wanted to lay it out to be sure we had not missed anything.

Dutch, Zehai and I carried everything into the map room and began to go over the case from the IG report through the findings from the gas company today. About half way through we ordered out from the TOP 5 NCO Club. They had an old Volkswagen van that made deliveries on post. We ate the hamburgers and cold French fries and worked through everything. About 9:30 P.M. Dutch called Mr. Barkus and told him what was going on and invited him for a briefing. Mr. Barkus and Colonel Nestler arrived about 45 minutes later. Dutch took the floor and briefed the case in detail. Mr. Barkus had a couple of questions, as did Colonel Nestler. All were answered with satisfaction.

Mr. Barkus said, "Sounds good. Oil up your handcuffs and make some reservations with the MPs for jail space."

Colonel Nestler then said, "Don't worry about jail space, these guys have priority. You guys did a fine job, sounds like general court—martial time to me." With that we broke up and headed home. I was feeling good and looking forward to the bigger meeting in the morning.

I was tired and it was all mental fatigue. Once back at the MP Company, I took a long, hot shower and was asleep the second my head hit the pillow. Tomorrow would be the adrenalin rush Dutch had talked about at the end of a big investigation.

# Chapter 9
## The Wheels Come Off

I woke up to a loud noise; somebody was banging on my door. I had not locked the door so in came the Midnight Shift Patrol Supervisor, Staff Sergeant Foreman.

"Green, there has been some kind of shooting downtown and you are wanted at the Provost Marshal Office ASAP."

I asked what happened and he said he did not know; he had just taken a radio call to get me.

"OK, Sarge, I'm on my way, thanks."

It felt like I had been asleep for about fifteen minutes but when I looked at my watch, 3:30 A.M. stared back at me. What is this about? My first thought was Giorgina. Had the three musketeers gone after her? No, that would not do them any good. Maybe it was not even related to the case. Some major event and there was an all-hands on deck call. I finished dressing and headed for the door, but felt sure it had to do with the case. I stopped, turned around and unlocked my footlocker. I took the .38 revolver Sergeant Tucker had given me and strapped it on under my shirt. Then I remembered what Sergeant Fisher had said; "There might be some ugly in this." I jumped in my car and headed across post to the Provost Marshal Office.

It was less than a five-minute drive and when I got there I noted that I was late for the party. All the lights were on and MP cars, CID cars and a couple of POVs (namely Colonel Nestler's and Sergeant Tucker's), surrounded the building. There was no place to park, so I parked next door in the Finance Office parking lot. Just as I was getting out of my car, Dutch drove in and parked. He did not know what was going on either. He had been asleep in his room in the BOQ when the night houseboy woke him up with a message to go to the PMO.

We walked in the building and I took in the crowd: Lieutenant Colonel Nestler, Mr. Barkus, Sergeant Tucker, Tim Wallace, Larry Higgins, Sergeant Foreman and four uniformed MPs (one my buddy Dan Neels). Mr. Barkus was a big man with a barrel chest. His voice matched his physique. He began to speak; there was no "At Ease" or "Give Me Your Attention". When he cleared his throat for the first word, you could hear a pin drop.

"For the late arrivals, a bit of history. Dutch and Joe have been working on a theft case for a couple of months. Fuel has been stolen or fraudulently diverted via false delivery orders from the motor pool for about a year and a half. It looks like three military members and one local national were involved. We were set to make the apprehensions in the morning, but there is a snag. The local national delivery driver who is involved was killed tonight. Shot in his house less than an hour ago." Just then Zehai and Adonay walked in the front door. Mr. Barkus gestured to them and asked what they found out downtown.

Zehai drew a breath to speak but Adonay already had several words in the air. He related that someone had shot the driver and his wife through an open window as they slept in their small apartment. He said it looked like it had been a .22 rifle as they found nine shell casings on the ground outside the window. A neighbor had heard the shots and gone to investigate, finding the couple dead. He had then gone a couple of blocks and called the police. Adonay said he had been routinely notified; then, when he heard the name, he contacted us.

Mr. Barkus then detailed what we would do. He said that we had to move immediately to arrest our three suspects and search their homes and cars for evidence of the shooting. He then rattled out the plan as if he had been working on it for a week. He assigned Dutch, me, Zehai and Adonay to arrest Captain Watson. We were to drive directly to his off-post residence, take him into custody and remove his family from the home. A uniformed MP and an Ethiopian policeman would secure the home until Adonay could obtain a civilian search warrant.

Tim Wallace and two MPs would go to Falk's on-post quarters, take him into custody, remove his family from the home and stand by until search authority was obtained. Larry Higgins and two uniformed MPs would go to Lucas' on-post quarters and do the same. Mr. Barkus said he would wake up the Installation Commander and obtain the search authority for the two on-post government quarters and the work areas of the suspects. All three suspects would be taken to the CID office and held separately until we began to question them. He then released us to begin.

I shot my eyes to Dutch, then looked at Dan Neels and raised my eyebrows. Dutch knew exactly what I was saying, and nodded. With that approval I grabbed Dan by the arm and said, "You're with us."

He smiled and said that he had been hoping for that. Dutch's CID sedan was up at the office, so I asked Dan if he had a car. "Yep" he said, "Like new, only 92,000 miles."

Kagnew Station was at the end of the supply line and the Military Police were at the bottom of the list for cars. So we tried our best to make them last, often difficult with car chases, bumpy roads and the heat of the desert. We walked outside and got into Dan's Ford. Dutch got into the back seat and told me to sit up front with Dan. We dropped Zehai and Adonay at the CID Office to get Dutch's sedan. We would need some more space before the night was over.

Dan drove out the gate and down the hill at a nice clip, turning left at the traffic circle in front of the Fiat garage and heading to the Watson home in the Gheza Banda. Captain Watson lived about in the center of this residential section of Asmara, one of the nicer neighborhoods of mostly Americans, Italians and well-to-do natives. Just down the street from his house sat an Ethiopian police car with two policemen. We stopped behind the car and they quickly dismounted, hands on guns, not realizing who we were. They recognized the marked Military Police car and relaxed a bit. Adonay quickly came up and directed them to the backside of the residence. We then walked to the front door. Dan, in uniform, was in front, followed by Adonay with Dutch and me behind. Dan knocked on the door. There was no response and the house was dark. Dutch then took his flashlight and rapped smartly on the door about a half-dozen times. A light came on and then a couple of minutes later Captain Watson came to the door.

I took him in, all of him. He had sleep in his eyes and looked like he had genuinely just been awakened. He had a line across his face as if he had been sleeping on a fold in the pillowcase. I looked at his ankles and feet. He had kind of fat legs and ankles. No sock marks. Yep, this guy had been in bed and asleep for awhile, not pacing the floor after just shooting somebody. But nevertheless, we took him into custody. Dutch informed him of his status and read him the Article 31 warning. Dan cuffed him and marched him down to where the cars were parked.

Captain Watson had two cars inside his gate in his driveway. A US—made Mercury and a second car, a Fiat. I checked tires and hoods of both of the cars. They were cold; they had not been driven in some period of time. It sure didn't look like Captain Watson had been involved in tonight's shooting.

We loaded Captain Watson in the back of the CID car and drove him back to post. Dan followed with his wife and son. They went to the break room at the MP Station and we took the suspect to a holding room at the CID Office. Tim Wallace, who had Lieutenant Falks in another holding room, met us there. He gave us the same report; there was no initial evidence to put Falks out of the house in the past several hours. Then Larry Higgins came in with Sergeant Lucas. A bit of a different story.

Lucas had not been home and his wife had reported that he had gone running and then would go to the post swimming pool for his morning swim. Larry and one of the MPs had located him in the pool doing laps. He had been taken into custody. A nice swim in a chlorine pool would go a long way to removing gunshot residue from his skin. Larry added that his jogging clothes were wet with the smell of chlorine and hanging by the pool. He had washed them out in the pool water, too. My guess was he had drawn the short straw while Watson and Falks had a nice night's sleep.

We spent over five hours with the questioning of the three suspects. No confessions, no acknowledgements of anything to do with the theft, no nothings. They were not stupid. They had rehearsed their statements and were just different enough to not look like pat hands. With the search authorities in place, we broke off back to our three teams and searched their houses and cars. Again nothing. Like all soldiers they each had some guns. Neither .22 rifles nor any .22 caliber ammunition was located. Then it was to the Transportation Office and the Motor Pool. We searched their work areas, desks and the common areas of both places. Again nothing. We questioned the three men again in the afternoon and again, got nothing.

Dan Neels, Zehai and several other MPs, along with Adonay and some more of his people, had done a house-to-house check of the neighborhood in the Gheza Banda and on-post and were unable to find any witnesses that had seen the suspects out and around in the early morning hours. We met with two lawyers from the Staff Judge Advocate and learned officially what we already knew. We had nothing but circumstantial evidence. Without the statement of the driver we were hamstrung. Our strongest evidence was the delivery sheets. But they were not even in English. Lucas said he had signed the forms really not knowing what they were. A Letter of Reprimand for dereliction of duty at best. We had no choice but to release the suspects.

We released them and ordered from the Top Five NCO Club. We all sat in the map room with cold hamburgers and cold French fries and went over the case again. Dan Neels had stayed with us all day. He looked tired; heck, everybody looked tired. We could not find anything we had missed nor any further leads to pursue.

We would get a couple of the shell casings and one of the bullets from the driver's body and send it to the CID crime lab, then on to the FBI lab to see if the gun had been used in any other crimes that might possibly be associated with any of the three suspects. But we knew that would be a stretch. The gun was something that had been locally obtained on the gray market. This case would be open for a long time.

# Chapter 10
## Back On The Beat

It didn't end the way Dutch and I had planned; it didn't end good, but it ended. On the plus side were many things: we had worked hard and I learned so much and I gained a friend for life in Dutch. Although we never got the big adrenalin rush, we did have fun working on the case. But we knew the three were walking around with a big fat smirk on their faces and holding some profits from the fraud. It was as plain as the nose on your face, but it just could not be proven.

Mr. Barkus called Dutch and me into his office just before quitting time on my last day on the detail. He thanked me with a lot of sincerity and complemented me on my hard work. He presented me with a very nice CID Command Certificate of Achievement signed by the Provost Marshal General.

Then he said some warming words; "Dutch, your job is to get Joe's signature on an application to CID School. You guys know I got a Rabbi that will make it happen."

We all smiled, then began to laugh. It had been a good two months working with CID. I would miss it, but I was looking forward to climbing back into one of those 85,000 mile Fords and getting back on the road. Then Mr. Barkus said that he was hungry. We walked into the map room and the table was set for dinner. All the guys were there with their wives or girlfriends and then I saw Giorgina helping Adriana with the dinner. I knew it would be a good evening, and it was.

The next morning I checked in with Sergeant Fisher and he said to take the weekend off and start back on the shift on Monday. That was nice, a weekend off. I had not had one of those in a while. We had worked most Saturdays and even after the shrimp boils we had gone over the case for an hour or two. Free time would be nice.

Giorgina and I spent Saturday on a little ride down the Massawa Road to Nefasit. We had lunch in an Eritrean restaurant, then a nice slow ride back up the hill with a couple of stops for coffee and picture—taking. We met Dutch downtown for dinner. Dutch was relaxed. We talked shop for a bit, and then movies that were out and Dutch surprised me by starting a conversation about popular music. We had our coffee at the bar and were out of the restaurant by 10:00 P.M. Giorgina and I drove out to lookout point and talked for a bit; I had her home just before 11:30 P.M.

The next few months were the norm: patrols, dates with Giorgina, hanging out with Dutch and helping him a bit on my time on my days off. I don't know if I enjoyed the investigative work or being with Dutch. Then one Monday morning the houseboy woke me up and said to call CID. I called Dutch and he said he had some news to share. I drove up to his office and he handed me stack of papers with one of those big Army staples through it. It was orders for his reassignment back to the states. He was going to the CID office at Fort Gordon, Georgia. He was a short-timer already. His Fort Gordon reporting date was in 20 days! He was not happy, but said that it was a bit better than Vietnam. We laughed and he grabbed the cup of coffee that I had with me. Then we really laughed.

That made me think. My thirty-six months would be up in just a couple of more months. What was in store for me? Vietnam always needed MPs. Maybe I could get a good assignment there and then work my way back to Asmara. One day I would have to come to grips with Giorgina. People said we were like an old married couple. Yes, we felt very comfortable together and really liked the same things. But was it love or just two people that just got along great? I didn't know what love was. There were too many things yet to do before I settled into the routine of cutting grass on Saturday morning and then loading up to go to the Commissary. I just didn't feel like now was the time for that. Giorgina and I had never had any conversations about "us". It had been something I thought was a tomorrow topic. What did she think?

I didn't see Dutch for a couple of days, then one day I saw him walking down the street carrying a clipboard. That was the true sign of a short-timer, clearance papers on a clipboard. One went to all the facilities for final clearance. You got their stamp of initials showing you had turned in a library book, paid your club bill and closed your credit union account. And on it went, about 20-some different activities around post. The last one was military personnel where you turned in your clearance papers and picked up your 201 file to carry to your next duty station. I walked along with Dutch for a bit. He was not a happy camper. We stopped at the NCO Club and some coffee that was tuned up just a bit with brandy. We both laughed when Dutch said that really took the chill off the day. It was over 100—degrees and not yet noon.

The CID guys had Dutch's going-away party downtown at Cassidy's nightclub. There was a nice party room in the back and a good restaurant catered in a fine meal. Giorgina and I were invited. Colonel Nestler, Sergeant Tucker and their wives were also there. It was a really good evening. Dutch left two days later. As was the Asmara custom, all his friends went to the airport with him to get him on the freedom bird. We all sat up in the lounge and sipped Melotti beer until his flight was called. Dutch walked around shaking hands and giving hugs, then turned and walked towards his gate. About twenty feet away he stopped and turned around to waive. He had tears in his eyes. Asmara did that to all of us. It was a unique assignment.

With Dutch gone I felt really alone. I just had Giorgina close to me. It made me appreciate her all the more and, as I looked at the calendar, I knew that my day of reckoning was approaching. Then it happened. I walked in the MP Station for a midnight shift and Sergeant Fisher handed me a stack of papers with one of those big Army staples.

He smiled and said, "Well, short timer, this is your last night; you got a short fuse."

I looked at the orders; my permanent change of station departure flight was in eight days. Then I looked further and saw my new assignment was the 141st MP Company, Ft Gordon, GA. Was that a coincidence or did somebody have their Rabbi pull a string? I smelled my old friend! Well, well. In any event it was time for a cup of coffee with Dutch.

# Chapter 11

## Back To The World

I rode around on patrol that night and felt so alone. They didn't give me any calls, not even as backup. It was Friday night and there was a lot happening, but I was just not in the mood. That was fine; my mind was jumping all over the world. The night passed slowly. Then about 2:30 A.M., "Unit 28, this is Observer." It was Sergeant Fisher's voice. I answered and he called me to the station. I was not far away. I was there in less than five minutes, parked and walked into the desk area. There was Sergeant Fisher and Giorgina.

Sergeant Fisher said, "Turn in your stuff, Giorgina needs some help with a matter."

What the heck was that all about? I never ceased to be amazed at the lines of communication in Asmara! I closed out my trip ticket and gave the keys and paperwork to the Desk Sergeant along with my .45 and 21 rounds of ammunition.

Giorgina and I walked outside and she opened the door of my Fiat. There on the back seat was a bucket full of ice and a bunch of Melotti beer. We stopped at the MP Company where I changed clothes, then rode out to lookout point on the Massawa Road where we worked on the beer. We leaned back in the seats and drifted off to sleep reminiscing over the good times we had in Asmara. Neither of us brought up the "us" subject. Later I would understand that this was what her visit was all about. She did not want to be the one to bring it up, but she sure did everything possible to give me the opportunity. Many times later I would kick myself in the butt for not grasping it. The sun came over the mountain and into the car like a light coming on in a dark room. We both woke up and I drove down the mountain road a couple of kilometers to a restaurant that overlooked the valley far below. We sat out on the terrace and had fresh Italian rolls, ham, salami and cheese with cappuccino. It was a good breakfast and Giorgina sure looked good in the morning sun.

The next days went fast. I didn't have much but I did ship a couple of hundred pounds of hold baggage to Fort Gordon. I got my clearance papers and bought myself one of the famous Army clipboards, the sure sign of a short-timer as one walked around post from office to office. I stopped in the CID office to say good-bye to the agents. Mr. Barkus reminded me that he had several Rabbis on the bench and that all I had to do was say the word. No, it was time to get moving. Had it been anything but Fort Gordon it would have been a very tough call. I needed to talk to Dutch and figure out what direction to go: CID school, back to Asmara for Giorgina and bring her to the states, or just skip the grass cutting and trips to the Commissary? I didn't know where I was. Friday was my last night in Asmara. Sergeant Tucker and his wife invited Giorgina and me to dinner at the Top Five Club. He was a smart man and set an early time so that we could do what we wanted to do.

I had one last thing to do to finish my clearing. I went downtown to the Ethiopian traffic office and put my car into Giorgina's name with the taxes paid and put the nice new set of Ethiopian license plates on the car. She just loved my little Fiat and I knew that transportation would make life a lot easier.

I picked her up at the Provost Marshal Office at 5:00 P.M. for the last time. She jumped into the car and gave my arm her famous squeeze. She wanted to run home and change before we met the Tuckers at the club. When we stopped at her house, I asked if she noticed anything different about the car. She walked around and was only able to notice that it had been freshly washed and waxed. I pointed to the license plates and handed her the documents. The closest I could get to tell her that I would be back was saying, "Keep it waxed until I get back." She smiled and gave me her hug.

We had dinner with the Tuckers and Jack would not say good-bye or shake my hand. "See you tomorrow at the airport."

Giorgina and I rode around town for a couple of hours not knowing what to say or do. Finally, just before midnight, we wound up out at lookout point on the Massawa Road. We sat and talked. I told her that I would be back soon. I wanted to spend a bit of time with Dutch, take a couple of career-enhancing courses at the MP School, and then I would call upon some Rabbis and get back to Asmara. I told her that next summer I would send her a ticket and she could spend her vacation in America. I don't know what she thought; she said things like that will be nice and I'll be here when you get back, but neither of us seemed to be ready for some deep commitment. At least I wasn't and now, in retrospect, I think she was just going along with me.

As was always the case on lookout point, the sun popped over the mountain and bathed us in early morning light. No time for a nice leisurely breakfast. I had to be at the airport at 10:00 A.M. We drove back to post and Giorgina dropped me at the MP Company. She said she would be back at about 8:00 A.M. and we would make our way to the airport.

I walked into the MP Company for the last time. It had been my home for 36 months and I was not ready to leave. Questions arose: what would Fort Gordon be like, would Dutch and I have time to spend together, would I really feel comfortable there like I did here? I took my last long hot shower, finished packing and got dressed in some nice civilian clothes for the long ride to JFK, New York. I carried my duffle bag to the front door, then walked back to the orderly room and picked up my travel packet, official 201 file, red "Traveling Abroad on Official Business for The US Government" passport and a few bucks I had placed in the company safe.

I walked to the front of the MP Company and looked at my watch. It was 7:50 A.M. and there in the parking lot was Giorgina. Would I ever get to a meeting before her? Then it dawned on me. Just when and where would our next meeting be? I put my bag in the back seat and got into the car. She handed me a cup of coffee and we rode to the airport.

The Asmara airport was about 5 miles outside of town, but a 15-minute ride with the bicycles, pedestrians and gerry carts. We parked in the parking lot and I looked over at Giorgina. She was crying.

She said, "This will be our last time alone, Joe. Your gang will be inside for the Kagnew Station sendoff. I want you to know that I love you and whatever you do will be OK." With that she jumped out of the car and walked to the back of the car and worked on her makeup while I got my duffle bag out.

We walked inside and to the Ethiopian Airlines counter. I checked my bag and they looked at my passport and ticket. We walked upstairs and were met by about 35 people.

Sergeant Tucker, his wife, Mr. Barkus, Adrianna, several of the Agents, about 20 MPs and two of the houseboys from the MP Company were all there. Giorgina talked to Adrianna and I made the rounds for the big handshakes and hugs. I would miss these folks; all were friends and most I would keep up with for the rest of my life. No other Army assignment was ever like Asmara. It had a way of growing on you and bringing people together.

It was not long until I heard them call my flight. In a panic I scanned the crowd until I saw Giorgina over by herself. I made my way to her and we hugged. Not her little patented hug, but a nice long hug until I heard them say "final call". I gave her a long kiss and said my good-bye. I turned and started walking to the gate. Then I remembered Dutch. I stopped, turned, and with tears in my eyes, waved to the crowd. Just before the gate I turned and took one last look at Giorgina. She was waiving and crying. That memory would stay with me forever.

I got on the Ethiopian Airlines Boeing 707 and found my seat, a window seat on the left side just behind the wing. There were not too many on the flight so the other two seats were empty. That would be good. I would not be ready for conversation for awhile. They closed the door and the plane moved down to the taxiway. As it turned onto the taxiway I got a look back at the terminal. Everybody was out on the balcony waiving. I could not see Giorgina.

The pilot didn't stop the jet when he turned onto the runway; he just gave it the gas and away we went. It quickly climbed to about 3500 feet then made a slow left turn. I looked out the window and saw Kagnew Station between the clouds. I was able to pick out the MP Station and the PMO. Then it was gone, covered by the clouds. And, I too, knew I was gone. It was not a good feeling.

# Chapter 12

## *Stateside Duty*

It was a long trip. The Ethiopian airliner took me to Athens via Cairo. I spent the night in Athens, then the next morning it was TWA nonstop to JFK, New York. From New York I flew to Ohio and spent a week with my brother on his farm. I helped out with some bailing of wheat straw, visited some old high school friends, and then that next Saturday I flew to Columbia, South Carolina and caught a military bus from Fort Jackson on to Ft Gordon, GA. It was the third week of September but it was hot. For a while I thought I was back in Africa.

The Army bus out of Fort Jackson had a bunch of recruits on their way from basic training to the MP School. I was in uniform so I could realize the military travel rate on the flight from Ohio to South Carolina. Once the recruits learned that they had a genuine MP with them, I answered questions for the entire 200-mile trip. Kind of fun; then about 5:00 P.M. we rolled up to the front gate of Fort Gordon. The MP on the gate was sharp and he allowed the bus to slow, took a look inside and waived us through. We stopped at the on-post bus station and a sergeant grabbed up the recruits like a mother duck getting her flock together. He had them lined up and getting on another bus before you could blink. He walked past me, noted my cross pistols MP collar brass and asked if I needed a ride to the school. I told him I was going to the

141st MP Company and he grabbed my duffle bag and headed to the bus, telling me it was right on the way.

The bus stopped in front of three World War II wooden barracks buildings and a smaller wooden building with a big sign out front identifying the area as the 141st Military Police Company. I thanked the driver and the Sergeant and walked into the orderly room. The Charge of Quarters was a buck sergeant that looked like he was fifty years old. I gave him a copy of my orders and he signed me in the company book. He handed me a ring with two keys on it and said that the First Sergeant had me in room 17 in building three. He pointed to one of the three barracks buildings and said that it was on the second floor.

I grabbed my duffle bag and headed to my new home. The room was OK. It had a good view across the post. There was an "Air Force" style bed, bigger than the hated Army bunk, a small desk, dresser and closet. I'm thinking this is rather nice for pay grade E-4. Just then there was a knock on the door. I opened the door and there was a man of about 35 years old in a sports jacket and slacks. He stuck out his hand and introduced himself as the First Sergeant. He welcomed me to Fort Gordon and the 141st MP Company.

"Sergeant Green, I came to see you today so that you would not be out of uniform when you report to the Commander Monday morning. We got a message from your old command that you came down on promotion orders a couple of days after you departed. This is not the most stunning of promotion ceremonies, but congratulations."

He handed me a stack of the promotion orders, several sets of Sergeant chevrons and a stack of 3D Army shoulder patches. He then said that we could go for a quick ride and he would get me orientated to the post. We got into his private car and did a quick tour. He pointed out the PX, a sewing shop that was open 7 days a week, the mess hall, the NCO Club and the snack bar. He then dropped me back at the MP Company and departed with a solid handshake, telling me to stop by the orderly room Monday morning about 9:00 A.M. and I would meet the Commander and get in-processed.

Sunday I took some uniforms to the sewing shop and the lady was good enough to do two of them while I waited and promised the rest for the middle of the week. I walked to the PX and bought an iron and a couple of other items. I got myself a fresh haircut, then back to the company area where I spent the rest of the day working on the two uniforms, shinning boots and shoes and watching some TV in the company dayroom. The same sergeant had CQ again on Sunday. We talked a bit and he told me a lot about Fort Gordon. He locked up the orderly room, put a sign on the door that said he was in the mess hall and we walked to dinner.

The next morning I met the Company Commander and started my in-processing. The First Sergeant gave me a jeep to get around post. I didn't have too many places to in-process so it looked like an easy day's work. I had more than half of it done and looked at my watch. It was 11:30 A.M. and just then I passed a newer building in the middle of all of the older buildings. The sign on the front said "Fort Gordon CID". I whipped into the parking lot and locked the jeep with a chain through the steering wheel and seat frame to a padlock.

I walked in and was met by a receptionist. I asked directions to Mr. Driggers' office and quickly learned that I was not on Kagnew Station. After giving my name, rank, serial number and purpose of the visit, she called Mr. Driggers and informed him he had a visitor.

A couple of seconds later Dutch appeared. It was old home week. I was so glad to see him. We shook hands and walked back to his office. He noted my stripes and gave me a big pat on the back. We walked down to the small kitchen they had there and made some coffee. We spent the next hour catching up. Dutch said he knew a little Italian restaurant that had good pasta and that he would pick me up around 6:00 P.M. and we would go to dinner.

I finished in-processing in the afternoon and returned the jeep to the First Sergeant and turned in my papers. He said to meet him back at the orderly room in the morning and we would go down to the Provost Marshal Office and meet the folks there who would give me a duty assignment.

Dutch and I had dinner and talked well into the late evening. Dutch told me he was approaching his 29th year of service and was beginning to look for a civilian police job for a second career. He said he could pull the pin at any time and that staying the full thirty would not make much of a money difference. His last pay bump was over 28, so as soon as he found a good job he would be gone. He mentioned a small town of Hayesville down near Brunswick, GA, that he was leaning toward. It bordered Fort Stewart, GA, so a PX, Commissary and Hospital was close and it was just off the new interstate highway, I-95, that would eventually run all the way up and down the east coast. He said he was going to ride down one day and look it over before he turned in his application.

Gosh, I thought, here by the luck of the draw I wind up at the same duty station as Dutch and he is a short-timer again before I get both feet on the ground. He saw the look on my face and I guess he knew what I was thinking. He told me to relax; he had not come to any conclusions yet. We paid and departed the restaurant. Dutch dropped me at the MP Company. It had been nice having dinner with Dutch, but it made me miss Giorgina. So many times it had been the three of us having dinner. I had written Giorgina three letters since I left Asmara, but tonight before I went to bed, I wrote a really long newsy letter and told her about Dutch and our nice dinner. And I told her how much I missed her.

The next day the First Sergeant took me to the Provost Marshal Office. I met the Provost Marshal and his Operations Sergeant, Master Sergeant Meadowcroft. He said I had been assigned to Staff Sergeant John Briggs' shift. They were working the midnight shift this month. My position would be area supervisor. The patrol supervisor had overall responsibility. The post was divided into two sections with two area supervisors each responsible for four patrol areas. He told me to go up to the MP station tonight at about 11:00 P.M. and meet Sergeant Briggs, get his in-briefing and he would give me the schedule for his shift.

I got dressed about 10:00 P.M. in a clean uniform, but no MP gear. I got to the MP Station a bit before 10:30 P.M. and was directed to the patrol supervisor's office. I knocked on the door and Sergeant Briggs got up from behind the desk, shook hands and greeted me with a warm welcome aboard. He was a different cut than Sergeant Fisher. Young, not yet thirty, tall at maybe 6'03" with short blond hair. But one could tell quickly that he knew his stuff. He asked me to sit down by his desk and he started by telling me about himself. He then handed me a copy of the duty roster and briefly identified and spoke about each of the people he supervised. He said I would be replacing one of his sergeants that had come down on orders for Germany. I would have about 10 days to ride with him and get the lay of the land and the strengths and weaknesses of the MPs I would supervise. He said my days off would be Monday and Tuesday unless there was some event that required maximum personnel or supervision. He asked me to hang around until 11:30 P.M. for guard mount and briefing. My first night would be Wednesday.

Thus began my tour of duty with the MP Station, Fort Gordon, Georgia.

# Chapter 13

## Dutch Checks Out Of The Net

I rode with Sergeant Hardy for the 10 days as directed by Sergeant Briggs. Sergeant Hardy seemed like a good MP. He had previous assignments in Vietnam, Okinawa and Germany. Fort Gordon was his only stateside assignment and he said he could not wait to get back to Germany and have a good beer. He explained that the job was keeping an eye on the four two-man patrols in our half of the post. Listen to the radio and go to their calls that are felonies, domestic disturbances or something out of the ordinary. And do it without making them think you don't trust them to handle their calls.

It didn't take me long to get the hang of it. I quickly learned the men that needed little or no supervision and the ones that could not write a parking ticket without a supervisor. One evening, when we were on the 4:00 P.M. to midnight shift, Dutch showed up just before roll call and introduced himself to Sergeant Briggs. He asked if there would be an objection if he came down from time to time and rode with me for a couple of hours. Sergeant Briggs said he would be happy to have him anytime he wanted to ride.

Thus began the custom of Dutch riding with me for several hours every week or 10 days. It was not a party. Dutch had a sharp eye and often saw things that needed police action. Then too, as we rode along, we talked shop, points of law, police procedures and some of the old customs and history of the Military Police Corps. It was over a year and Dutch had not put in for his retirement. I asked him about it one day and he said that the Vietnam thing was causing a real shortage of CID Agents and he had been asked to extend. He put in for it and received a 12-month extension beyond thirty years. Interesting. I guess Dutch would be around for a while.

Giorgina and I wrote back and forth two or three letters a week. I sent the letters to her in an envelope to Sergeant Tucker at the Provost Marshal Office. The Ethiopian mail would be very slow. Just for fun I sent her a letter at her home address and it took 37 days to get there. That was for the birds. She started telling me about the troubles between the Eritrean Liberation Front and the Ethiopian Government. The ELF was ramping up civil war actions and talk in an attempt to gain Eritrean independence. She said it did not look good, and her father was very seriously thinking of moving the family back to Italy. She said Italians were leaving every day. In my next letter I told her that I would send her a ticket and she could come to the United States. She wrote back that it was very tempting but she needed to stay and help her family. Her mother's health was not great.

As the war picked up Kagnew Station fell out of favor with the local people. Kagnew had been a project of Emperor Haile Selassie and of course he was on the Ethiopian side of things. Several Americans were kidnapped and one MP was killed patrolling on the Massawa Road. Travel outside of Asmara was restricted by the command and the writing on the wall was that the days were numbered for Kagnew Station. Then in a flash Kagnew Station began a rapid drawdown. Dependents were sent home and the mission was vastly reduced. Then within a month the installation was closed and the lease returned to the Ethiopian government.

After that we had to use the civilian mail and I only got two more letters from Giorgina. They told of the war, the lack of services and the deteriorating health of her mother that made it impossible to travel. I continued to write every day for two months, not receiving any response. I contacted the American Consulate in Asmara asking for their help in locating Giorgina. I got a very nice form letter back stating that they were closing the Consulate and relocating personnel and records to the Embassy in Addis Ababa. They were sorry but they neither had the time nor facilities to inquire about the status of local nationals.

Dutch suggested that we try to contact Adonay and Zehai. We wrote several letters to Adonay at the Asmara Police Station but got no reply. Likewise letters to Zehai were not answered. The news told of terrible atrocities in Eritrea and I was left with the very worst of thoughts for Giorgina and her family. I followed the news as best as I could. It was not a major topic in the United States. But I was able to track that the war was dragging along at a snails pace with neither side seeming to gain advantage. They would fight like crazy for a couple of months, then abandon their positions and move their forces across the country. No real rhyme or reason.

Dutch and I became very close. One weekend we visited Hayesville, Georgia, and found it to be a very nice little town. They had a small, but what appeared to be, an efficient police department. We went in and met the Chief, Bob Rainer. He said he was always looking for experienced officers, especially those with investigative experience. He opened his desk and handed Dutch an application. Dutch told him that he would stay in touch, but had about 10 months left on his hitch. Another time Dutch and I went up to the outer banks of North Carolina and did some serious deep-sea fishing. What a trip! We visited Savannah, Charleston, and Atlanta and toured all through Florida. We had some good times. Dutch got down to 5 months on his extension and told me one day he had sent his application to Hayesville. By this time I had been at Fort Gordon for almost two years. Vietnam was winding down and the Army was beginning to stabilize assignments. My guess was that I was good for at least another year. I would be able to attend another of Dutch's going-away parties.

Dutch continued to ride with me every week or so. One rainy night we had been at it for about three hours. We had ridden a couple of calls with the beat patrols and even answered a loud party call ourselves. I told Dutch that the PX Gas Station was just up the road and it looked like time for a coffee break. Yep, he was ready. We pulled in and parked on the side of the parking lot so as not to tie up a parking space for customers. We were walking to the store when a guy came running out carrying a plastic bag and a gun. He took one look at me in MP uniform and raised his gun to me. As I drew my .45, Dutch stepped in front of me and fired three times. I got off two shots. The robber shot twice. The whole thing didn't last 5 seconds. The suspect and Dutch both fell to the ground. I looked down at Dutch. He was holding his stomach with both hands. The suspect was on the ground but his gun was within reach of him. I walked over and looked at him. He was dead; at least four rounds had hit him.

I ran back to Dutch. He had taken one right in the gut. He pulled me to him and said, "This isn't good. I got it right there in Korea and it's all plastic and mesh. Shit."

I screamed for somebody to call an ambulance. Two soldiers came over and said one was on its way and what could they do. I ordered up some towels and told them to make it fast. Just as they were turning, Dutch raised his hand and pointed, "And a cup of coffee, black please."

I had my hand pressing on his stomach. Blood was pouring out with a gurgling sound. He didn't have long and he knew it. The soldiers came back with towels and some gauze pads from the store stock and the cup of coffee for Dutch. I took the towels and opened Dutch's shirt and tried to stop the bleeding. It slowed a bit but that was only because he was running out of blood. Dutch took a sip of the coffee, and then set it down with his hand still around it. His last words were, "Thanks, Joe, thanks for the years." He was gone.

The years flashed by: Dutch grabbing the first cup of coffee, the three of us—Dutch, Giorgina and me at dinners, Dutch in his garden, the shrimp boils, Dutch coming around the corner in his right-hand drive Fiat, Dutch at his desk meticulously studying a case file, the hunting trips in Africa, the travels in the states, and his soft spoken words, always putting you first. And then I snapped back and began to cry. I looked down at Dutch. He was gone. My best friend ever; a brother, a buddy and a father, all in one. The years ahead would never be the same. I laid his head on the towels, pulled his eyes shut and stood up. Hell, he was still holding the coffee and had not spilled a drop. That was Dutch. I took the coffee from his hand and began to drink it. It was about time I took his coffee.

The sirens got closer. Soon the parking lot was full of MP and CID cars and ambulances. Dutch's partner, a young CID agent, walked up and looked down at Dutch. He too was crying. I looked at the other agents; all had tears in their eyes. There would never be another Dutch. God just made one of him.

A few days later I was called to the Staff Judge Advocate Office to see one of their attorneys. I met the man, Captain Jenkins, and he advised me that I was the sole beneficiary of Dutch's estate. He did not have much: a car, a small bank account, a small IRA and life insurance for his final arrangements. The attorney then handed me a sealed envelope with my name on the outside. It was from Dutch asking for me to handle his arrangements. He wanted a very small service in the post chapel, and then he wanted to be cremated. He asked that I spread his ashes on a beach on a nice sunny morning. The attorney then gave me a large envelope with Dutch's effects and the keys to his room in the BOQ.

I thanked him and drove to the post Chaplain and made the funeral arrangements. Next it was over to Dutch's room to get a suit or uniform for the service. His room was rather Spartan: a TV, small refrigerator, a nice comfortable bed, dresser, a desk, some end tables and chairs. I opened his closet and there were two Army green uniforms hanging up. Both had highly shined brass and all the patches and ribbons. I had never seen Dutch in uniform. I looked at the uniform and noted the rank insignia of Master Sergeant. I knew he had been Sergeant First Class in Asmara. He had been promoted and did not tell me, another instance of not wanting to be in the spotlight. I then looked at his ribbons. He had five rows of ribbons: two silver stars, a soldier's medal, two meritorious service ribbons, a bronze star with V device, and three purple hearts. Even in death Dutch amazed me. I found his shirt, tie, belt, shoes and socks and took them back to the Chaplin.

It was a simple ceremony attended by all from the CID Office, the Provost Marshal Office and about 45 MPs and CID Agents, mostly officers and NCOs, from the MP Company and MP School along with some brass from CID Headquarters in Washington. Later I went back to his room to start clearing things for the return of the room to the BOQ. The thrift shop picked up the furniture and I directed that the proceeds be sent to Army Emergency Relief. I kept his papers, books and personal items. I boxed them up and thought this will be good reading someday. I did not want to get into it just now. I turned the room in and received a check for $247.00. Dutch was paid up two months in advance.

The next day I received a call from the post mortuary that Dutch's ashes were ready to be picked up. I went downtown to a funeral home and purchased a nice urn for Dutch. It might be just a while before I would find a beach and a sunny day. I then picked up Dutch and drove to the drive-up window at the snack bar and got two cups of coffee. I parked near the parade field and Dutch and I had our last coffee together.

# Chapter 14

## The Years Move Along

I had been right on the permanent change of station moves. Once Vietnam shut down people could not get moving even if they had the Chief Rabbi on their team. Guys coming back from Vietnam were filling all the vacant slots and nobody else was moving. I spent 2 more years at Fort Gordon. I got comfortable and kind of came to like the place. I made a trip to Hayesville and met with Chief Rainer. He expressed his condolences on the passing of Dutch. He then asked how much more time I had until retirement. I told him I had fifteen years in and he said to keep in touch, that Hayesville had a bunch of guys retiring along about then and he would save me a spot.

I knew that Hayesville would be my new home. I just had to get Dutch out of that bottle and get him some fresh air. It was a nice sunny day just like he had ordered. Hayesville was just 15 or so miles from the coast. I had brought Dutch with me thinking this would be the time. I drove to the ocean and turned down the coast road. I would know it when I saw it. Then just a few miles down the road I found the perfect spot. No houses for a good mile in either direction and a big expanse of white sandy beach. I got Dutch out of his case and walked down the beach. The sun was high in the sky and warm on my face. Yes. I opened the urn and let Dutch blow into the wind. It was a special swirl that took him high up in the air, then down across the sand just at the water's edge.

"Enjoy the beach, old friend. I'll be back from time to time."

I used my time at Fort Gordon to go over to the MP School and take a few career-enhancing courses. The MP Company was very good about giving me the time. Sergeant Briggs left for reassignment to Korea and I was put into the slot of Patrol Supervisor. Same money, but a lot more work. Then to my utter surprise, I was promoted to Staff Sergeant a month later. I wished Giorgina could have been there for the ceremony. It was very nice. The Army does a fantastic job on promotions and awards. I kind of gave up on the CID school idea. I was moving along rather well and I did like the daily dose of adrenalin. CID would just not be the same without Dutch.

During Vietnam the forces in Europe had been ripped off to support Southeast Asia. It was time to strengthen Europe as the Soviet Union began to flex its military strength. A lot of guys were being sent to Germany and I had been at Fort Gordon pushing five years. My number was up. Sure enough, no sooner did I start to figure this out than I walked in the orderly room one afternoon and the First Sergeant handed me a stack of papers with one of those big Army staples through it.

"OK, where am I going"? I asked without looking.

"Well, Joe, you are going on vacation. The 385th MP Battalion in Nuremberg. If you get rolling, you can make October Fest." We laughed and I wondered if I still had my clipboard.

The 385th MP Battalion had MP Stations all over southern Germany but I didn't get too far. I was assigned duty as Desk Sergeant in the Main MP Station, Nuremberg. The city was hopping in those days. We put out upwards of 15 patrols on the afternoon shift and a good 12 on the other two shifts. Never seemed to have enough either. My job was to manage the radio operators, desk clerks, walk-in complaints, and approve MP reports. It was 8 hours of non-stop action. I missed the road, but the desk was interesting. The radio never shut up. If it was not Nuremberg traffic, then it was radio traffic from other MP Stations within radio range. All 56 reporting MP Stations in Germany, the three in Italy, and only God knows how many sub-stations were on the same frequency. Sometimes late on a clear night, when things quieted down on the radio, you could sometimes hear Verona, Italy. Verona had a civilian Italian female radio operator. When she was on the air I would give the radio both ears. Her soft-spoken English with the Italian accent reminded me so much of Giorgina. The guys soon noticed this and suggested I take leave, go to Verona and meet her. I was not interested in that, but it did give me an idea.

If Giorgina and her family had gotten out of Asmara, they would be in Italy. I had tons of leave backed up on the books. I always saved as much as I could, and then cashed it in at reenlistment time. It made a nice little bonus along with the standard re-up pay. I met with the Station Commander, First Lieutenant Leslie Bailey, and he approved my 15 days leave. His nickname was "Nubs", but of course nobody called him that to his face. He had the two joints of the last two fingers missing on his left hand. The story was that as a young civilian policeman in Reno, Nevada, Nubs and his partner had gotten into a fight over who would drive the patrol car. Nubs got cut when his partner threw him through the door glass of the police car.

I packed some clothes, jumped in my nearly new BMW and headed to Garmisch and over the Austrian Alps to Italy. Once down the mountain road and into Italy, I felt so at home. It was my first time in Italy but I was an old hand at the language, architecture and customs. I figured I would go to the Italian Red

Cross in Rome and maybe the Eritrean embassy and I might be able to find some information.

As I rode along the Italian Autostrade, I looked at the map and noted that the Autostrade ran right through Verona. Curiosity was getting the best of me. Wonder what the sexy voice at the MP Station looked like? I thought I would pay the MP Station a courtesy call and find out. And, after all, I would have to report to the guys back in Nuremberg. I looked at the map and my watch. I would be getting to Verona about 5:00 P.M. It would be a good place to hold up for the night.

I arrived in Verona and got directions to Boscomantico, the Army installation where the MP Station was located. I made my first stop at the MP Station for a look-see and some information. The Desk Sergeant was a young buck sergeant who was full of information. He pointed me to the guesthouse and a good downtown restaurant close to the post. I looked into the small radio room just off the desk area and noted an MP private working the radio. I asked the Desk Sergeant about the soft Italian voice that we heard up in Nuremberg from time to time. Laughing, he said, "Oh, you must mean Rosa. You just missed her; she is on days this month. She comes in about 7:30 A.M. in the morning."

I thanked him for the information and headed to the guesthouse. I could not figure out what he thought was so funny.

I got a room and then followed his directions to the restaurant he had recommended. It was very good food, but not a good time. There I was in a nice Italian restaurant eating a great plate of pasta but missing Giorgina and Dutch. Sometimes life is so unfair. I tossed and turned all night and woke up early, too early to see Rosa. Hum, I made an excuse to myself and walked to the mess hall and had a nice breakfast. Back to the guesthouse, checked out and over to the PX gas station to fill up at US Forces prices. Italian gas prices were outrageous. All my lollygagging had paid off; it was 7:45 A.M. I drove over to the MP Station. One should thank them for their help. The day shift Desk Sergeant gave me a nice good morning and asked what he could do for me.

"Nothing thank you, I'm Sergeant Green on leave from the 385th MP Battalion and just wanted to thank you guys for last night's hospitality before I head out to Rome."

He smiled saying, "Anytime Sarge, stop in on your way back through."

I smiled, thanked him and peaked into the radio room. Sexy voice Rosa, all 375 pounds of her, was busy on the radio sending a patrol on some type of call. Yep, I would definitely have a report for the guys back in Nuremberg.

I drove onto Rome arriving in the city center about 3:30 P.M. I found myself a small hotel off the beaten path at a good price that also had parking. It was within an easy walk of Via Veneto and the US embassy. I would make the embassy my starting point.

I arrived at the embassy the next morning and spent a good hour dealing with red tape and answering questions before I got to anybody that could or would talk to me. I spoke with a young counselor affairs officer who, as I knew, had no information on Italian nationals or local national employees of the former Kagnew Station. He said most records maintained by Kagnew had been burned as they made their hasty exit from the country. A few records had been sent back to the State Department but he said these would only be employment and pay histories. There had been no tracking of local nationals as the post closed. He gave me directions to the Italian Red Cross who would have records of those Italians that had returned during that time in a refugee status. He said that the affairs of Eritrea were being maintained by the Israeli embassy because of the large number of Jews in Eritrea.

Eritrea did not yet have an embassy in Rome. Door number one had no prize.

I walked back to my hotel and got my car. The Red Cross was across town. I fought my way through the Rome traffic and made the 12 miles in just less than two hours. I would not like to live in this town. The Red Cross had several desks in the lobby and each had a small sign. I got into the line that indicated "Refugee Information". After about twenty minutes I was talking to an older Italian woman who spoke perfect English. I explained my problem and gave her a typed sheet of paper with all the information I knew about Giorgina and her family. She got up from her desk and walked through a door and came back about 15 minutes later with only my sheet of paper. She had no information at all on the family but recommended that I go to the Italian bank that handles retired pay for Italian soldiers. She gave me the bank name and directions. Door number two had no prize.

The bank was right downtown within walking distance of my hotel. So back through the traffic I drove. I parked and walked the 10 or so blocks to the bank. I thought that they would not want to give any information, especially to an American trying to do no more than find an old girlfriend. No, they were very helpful and immediately initiated a records search. After a rather long wait the clerk came back and reported that Giorgina's father had passed away in Africa a few years ago. The Italian Army has no survivor's benefits, as does the American Army, so with his passing his file was closed and there was no current record of the family. There was also no listed cause of death that might answer a question. But the date of death was after the hostilities had died down a bit and that gave me some hope. Door number three had no prize.

It was approaching 5:00 P.M. and the bureaucracy of the day had taken its toll on me. And as Dutch would say, "This job don't pay overtime." Tomorrow was another day. A good Italian dinner and a full night's sleep would arm me for tomorrow.

I started the morning with rolls, cheese and coffee in the hotel. The Israeli embassy was at the foot of the hill just off Via Veneto. I had a nice walk in the cool morning. I arrived just after 9:00 A.M. and was promptly greeted by a young man in a rather expensive Italian suit. I explained my problem and he asked if they were Jewish. Learning they were not, he contorted his face, took my information paper and walked upstairs. He returned a bit later reporting that they had no information on the family but that they would prepare an inquiry and include it in the next pouch going to Asmara. He explained that their activity there was rather small, three people working out of a hotel room, but sometimes they did have time for things like this. He took my Nuremberg contact information and walked me to the street. I felt sure I would never hear from them again. Door number four had no prize.

I walked back up the hill in the direction of my hotel and the US embassy. I stopped at an outdoor café for espresso and mulled over my plight. I still had ten days left on my leave. A quick flight to Asmara, three or four days on the ground, then back to Italy and drive back to Nuremberg. But I had a couple of problems. My DA Form 31, Leave and Pass Authority, indicated only travel to Italy. I go stumbling into Africa and something doesn't go right, I'm in an AWOL status. Some illness or injury occurs and it would not be in the line of duty. I could easily blow 16 years of working towards retirement. And I didn't have a passport, a necessary document for travel through Egypt and into Eritrea. Well, second things first. The Embassy is right up the street. Let's see just what it takes to get a passport.

I walked back to the embassy and located the same man I had talked to earlier. Since I had once had a passport, and an official passport at that, they could make me a passport by the close of business that day. But there was currently a travel ban on US citizens into Ethiopia and Eritrea. He said those bans come and go depending on the situation in the countries. I went ahead and had a passport made for some future travel as might be available. My second bang on door number one still did not give me a prize.

I had lunch, walked around Rome seeing the sights and tourist attractions, and then picked up my passport. I felt itchy and was ready to get on the move. Tomorrow would be a travel day.

I got up in the morning, had the continental breakfast in the hotel and got on the road. I had no idea where I was going. I looked at the map and plotted a course back to Germany. I would take the SS-1 up the west coast of Italy, see Pisa, go on up to Genoa through Switzerland and back to Germany. It looked like a nice three or four day ride with plenty of new scenery that would give me something else to think about.

I got back to Nuremberg several days before my leave was up. I spent one day cleaning and having my car serviced and the second just laying around shinning shoes and ironing uniforms. Then I cut my leave short and was back to work. Good, the busy MP Station occupied my mind and got me into the work I loved so much. Troubles were still with me, but seemed at a manageable distance.

I called my contact in the Rome embassy from time to time. The travel ban got lifted, and then quickly slapped back on just a couple of weeks later. He advised that it was just not the place to go. Armed bands of civilians patrolled the streets with some kind of quasi—government authority. They detained any foreigners, searched them, took their money and held them for days without reporting to the police of their embassies. The city was without water and electricity a lot of the time. The embassy staff was just a few people and unable to provide a lot of assistance to American citizens. It was just not the place to go. I tried to put matters further into the back of my mind. Maybe someday something would happen. Maybe.

The years flew past with not much change in Africa. I was fast approaching 36 months in Germany and would soon be returning to the states. I was approaching 18 years of service and thinking about that nice little town in south Georgia. I didn't have any Rabbis left. They had all retired. It was just me and the luck of the draw. I didn't even put in a dream sheet. You could put in a reassignment preference but they were never worth a hoot anyway. I'll just take what I get.

Then just about the time I thought it would happen, it did. I got a call to go to the orderly room to see the First Sergeant. There he was, holding that stack of papers and the dreaded giant Army staple. Wonder where I was headed? He handed them to me with a smile. On top was a sequence number from a Department of The Army centralized promotion selection to Sergeant First Class. He said it's a low number and you should be promoted in the first go-around in a couple of weeks. Second was reassignment to the 759th MP Battalion, Ft Dix, New Jersey.

The First Sergeant told me that it would be an interesting assignment. The 759th was a STRAF MP Battalion garden-plotted in the First Army area with a mission to respond to civil disturbances and disasters. He told me that more than likely I would be a platoon sergeant in one of the line companies. It would be lots of training and a good bit of travel. I was not in a rush mode this time; my reporting date was not for 60 days.

I spent a lot of those days realizing that New Jersey would put me further from Africa. I called my contact at the embassy and he again reported the travel bans were in effect and no sign of relief. Well, the years had passed with no news from Giorgina. I was finally coming to grips with what could be the worst of the possibilities. The news had reported hundreds of deaths in Asmara alone. I went to church that Sunday for the first time in a long time. I prayed for her and her family.

A couple of weeks later I got promoted to Sergeant First Class, E-7. One of the policies of the US Army Europe Provost Marshal was that no MP in the grade of E-7 or above would work shift work. So I was unemployed. I had less than a month until my flight back to the states so the First Sergeant gave me my clearance papers and told me to take my time. I dug through my stuff and found my well-traveled clipboard and started down the trail of installation clearance. I got up in the morning, had coffee with the First Sergeant, then went out and cleared an activity or two. Then I would go to the library, sign out a good book and spend the rest of the day reading. It took me 14 books to clear post.

# Chapter 15

# All Good Things Must Come To An End

The freedom bird was an Air Force C-141 from Rhein Main Air Force Base to McGuire Air Force Base. McGuire and Dix share a common boundary with several gates that connect the two installations. So arrival at McGuire was a cab ride to my new assignment. I got to the 759th MP Battalion just a bit after lunch and reported to the Battalion Headquarters. The acting Battalion Sergeant Major was a First Sergeant Welton Chase. He would later be my first sergeant in the 412th MP Company. First Sergeant Chase got me signed in and drove me to the Special Troops Bachelor Enlisted Quarters. Not too far from the MP Battalion. I got settled and he asked me to come back in the morning to get started on the in-processing.

In-processing took a couple of days and then I was assigned to one of the companies, the 412th MP Company, as the third platoon sergeant. I had a good group of guys, almost all of them were fresh out of MP School with no bad habits. There were a few seasoned troops reporting in from other commands. Time moved right along. The troops pulled "white hat duty" at the MP station for

30 days, worked at the post stockade for 30 days, and then trained as a platoon for 30 days.

My life was easy when they were working. I would go by the MP Station every day or so and visit with the Operations Sergeant. He would advise me of any problem areas or training needs. I would then work on those areas with my squad leaders. Same story when they worked the stockade. During the 30-day training cycle, it was more like basic training. Reveille at 6:00 A.M., barracks inspection, in—ranks inspection every Saturday morning and a full training schedule through the week.

We went through 5 or 6 of these ninety-day rotations and I stopped to realize that I was approaching 20 years. Twenty years is a 50-percent retirement; then it graduates up a bit each year until the maximum of 75 percent at 30 years. I was not a 30-year man. A twenty-year retirement would give me a nice monthly check while I was still young enough to start a second career, buy a house and have some type of a normal life without having to pick up and move every 3 years or so. Early on I had enjoyed the moving, travel and seeing different parts of the world, but now I was ready to throw out my anchor. Hayesville, Georgia, was looking really good.

I applied for and received 15 days of leave. A nice leisurely drive down I-95 put me in Hayesville in two easy days. Bob Rainer was still the Chief of Police. I told him I would be available in less than 90 days and he said that I was hired. Just like that. He gave me an application to fill out, stating it was a city hall requirement and then looked at his calendar and said, "How does November 1st sound?"

I told him, "Great, I will be in touch and settled in town a few days before November 1st."

I drove down the coast road and briefed Dutch. I told him I would be back for good shortly and we would have some coffee with brandy.

I spent a couple of days visiting with real estate agents and looking at apartments and smaller homes. It looked like it would be no problem finding something nice within my price range. I drove back to Fort Dix feeling that life was taking a good turn. Hum, grass cutting and trips to the Commissary. It sure would be fun with Giorgina.

I put my retirement in and received a retirement approval date of September 30th. I dug through my stuff and found the clipboard. It was older now and had nicks and cuts in it. I remembered the day I had bought it at the PX on Kagnew Station so many years back. But it was serviceable and it did its last job. I cleared post in a day and was ready to go. Fort Dix was a basic training post so they made a big deal of retirements. The last Friday of the month they had a parade and all the retirees for the month lined up on the parade field and received their retirement awards from the Commanding General. That Friday I was in the third row back behind officers and non-commissioned officers senior to me. The General trooped the lines, stopping at each retiree. He pinned a meritorious service ribbon on my green jacket, shook my hand, returned my salute and moved on to the next man. In all of 15 seconds twenty years was finished. The formation was dismissed and the retirees walked to their wives and children. I walked into the crowd and Welton Chase gave me a hug and a handshake. He wished me well and we parted company. I walked on to my car thinking even more of Giorgina. I had packed my car before the parade, so I headed off-post and was southbound on I-95 within the hour.

I got to the Philadelphia exits and turned west on the Pennsylvania Turnpike. I would visit my brother in Ohio for a week or so, and then make it to Georgia. The second half of my life lay in front of me.

# Chapter 16

## Starting Over Again

I spent two weeks at my brother's house, and then began to feel the travel bug. I said my good-byes and headed out early one morning. It was a two-day trip, I-75 south to Macon, Georgia, I-16 east to Savannah, then I-95 south just a few miles to the Hayesville exit. Hayesville is about 13 miles off of the interstate. I settled into a motel and then made a call on Chief Rainer. He said that the first day of the next pay period was October 29th, so that would be my start date. I would need to go by city hall and do some paperwork, then drive to Savannah to buy my uniforms. He explained the officers owned their uniforms, firearm and ammunition, and received a monthly uniform allowance in addition to their salary. He also said that I would have to attend the eight-week Georgia police academy to be a certified Georgia police officer and have arrest powers. The next academy started the first week of November and I was enrolled. Things were happening fast, not the relaxed pace of the Army.

I got in-processed at city hall, drove to Savannah and purchased my uniforms, and then to the tailor shop for patches and fitting. I purchased a nice Smith and Wesson 357 similar to what most of the other guys had. I had a few days until I went on the payroll, so I hung around the Police Department meeting the guys and picking up some information on things. That's when I realized what a small world we live in. There were two guys in this small 30-man department with whom I had been in the Army. I had met Joe Lane at Fort Dix, New Jersey and Jimmy Waynick in Germany. It was nice to see a familiar face.

I went on the payroll but just continued to hang around the Department. Read the SOP and officially met the supervisors and most of the guys. I started the 8-week academy in Savannah on November 4th. It was a gentleman's course that started every day at 8:30 A.M. and let out at 5:00 P.M. No barracks requirements or such, so I drove each day from Hayesville to Savannah. About a 40-mile trip one way. The eight weeks went by fast. There was not too much new material. Police doctrine and procedures are pretty much the same everywhere, but of course the Georgia laws were a new area. I graduated number two in the class of 35 guys. Number one was a prior civilian policeman attending from the Savannah Police Department who had been out of work long enough that he needed re-certification, so I didn't feel too bad.

I started work on Sergeant W.R. Jackson's shift. He was a knowledgeable laid-back guy who did not believe in over-supervision but did keep an eye on things. He reminded me very much of Jack Fisher. Hayesville was not the 15 two-man patrols of Nuremberg. We put out SGT Jackson and three one-man patrols, one in each of the three patrol areas. If nobody was sick, in school or on vacation, then we might have a fifth guy who would rove the three patrol areas to help out as needed. Then sometimes, when things were tight, there would be three of us and SGT Jackson would have to work one of the patrol areas. Things were generally quiet but there would be a hot call or two every once in a while, especially on paydays and weekends. After 20 years of nonstop adrenalin, I was ready for a few years of security checks, light calls and lots of time to drink coffee and chitchat with the citizens.

During my probation period I would pick up a car at the Police Department for each shift and then park it back there at the end of the shift. The station sergeant got those "pool" cars to the city garage for repairs and preventative maintenance. All I had to do was check the fluids and gas it up. After six months I came off probation and was assigned a take-home patrol car. That was nice. I was able to put my stuff in it and leave it. I didn't have to worry about what the last guy might have done to the car or that the next guy might complain that I had left it dirty or not serviced.

The car I was assigned was two years old but only had 22,000 miles. It had been one of the sergeants' cars and was reassigned out when he got a new one. I rode along fine for about three weeks and then noticed that it was due for an oil change and service. The requirement was that I take it to the city garage at the Department of Public Works and turn it in. My days off were Tuesday and Wednesday. So early on Tuesday morning I went to the garage to turn it in, hoping it would be back for duty on Thursday. I parked and walked in with the keys, asking for a work order sheet for the car. One of the mechanics directed me to the foreman's office to turn the car in. I walked in and could not believe my eyes. Sitting there in a nice white supervisor's shirt was the former Sergeant First Class Anthony Lucas from Kagnew Station.

The years had not been too good to him but I recognized him long before I looked at his nametag. I was quick to hold my expression and did not show any signs of knowing him. I said, "My name is Green and am assigned to Car 19. It's parked out there needing routine service. Do I write it up or what?"

He asked if there were any other problems. I told him it was just service, it was running like a top. He handed me a 5 x 8 card that needed to be filled out. It took me just a minute or two, and then I handed it back to him with the keys.

"OK, Green, give us 24 hours and you will be ready to go. Do you want to come get it or we can park it at the Department for you?"

I told him I'd be back mid-morning tomorrow and thanked him as I turned to leave. There was absolutely no indication that he remembered me. During his interview Dutch had done most of the questioning. I had spoken to him for a few minutes during a break and I had asked him some administrative questions. Dutch had been the one that kept him on the hot seat. That's who was burned into his mind.

I had rented an apartment that was about 10 blocks from Public Works, so I just walked home. I could not get Lucas out of my mind. Dutch always said, "Once a crook, always a crook". And, of course, we had pegged him as the triggerman on the shooting of the Ethiopian driver and his wife. I was getting real comfortable in south Georgia and now this had to come along.

# Chapter 17

## Seems Like We Have Been Here Before

This is not what I had expected. I was all set to do the very best job I could but I was not looking forward to dealing with Anthony Lucas again. Then I stopped to think. Were the other two scoundrels around here, too? I walked faster and then jogged the last three blocks to my apartment. Once inside I grabbed the telephone book. There they were. Watson and Falks were not five blocks away from each other. For the fun of it I looked up Lucas and he was right there within their circle. I still had Dutch's boxes. Several I had never opened. I started through his boxes and I found just what I was looking for, a page-by-page copy of the theft and murder case from Asmara. I started reading it. I read it at least four times, reading into the early morning.

I remembered again something that Dutch had told me, "Criminals are just like fishermen. If a fisherman catches a big one or has a good day, he will go right back to that same fishing hole the next time out. A crook makes a nice haul or fashions a good crime, he will repeat it." Where did the other two work? Did they too work for the city?

I could have called city hall and got the information in a flash. But I cautioned myself to go slow and keep my cards close to my vest. The first thing in the morning I got into my private car and drove over to the newspaper office. I asked if I could read some of the old newspapers. I was ushered into their library and shown the papers going back a couple of years with a name and event file. Look up the name or event and it would then reference in which edition you could find the person. Hayesville was a small town and just about everything was news, especially if it had to do with the city government. Watson and Flaks were referenced 10 or 15 times each. I pulled the papers out and learned the Watson was the Director of Public Works and Flaks was the city's purchasing agent. I could not believe that these three were up to their same old scam. I would have bet the ranch on it. But I could not go running down the hall of the police building shouting fire. I needed some facts. I didn't even have enough to go to our own detectives. I did not want to be accusatory to three senior city employees. I needed to come up with a plan.

I got back in my car and rode, a Dutch habit I had picked up, thinking good while riding around. Without thinking I wound up on the coast road. I came up to that beautiful expanse of white beach with nothing for a mile in either direction. I parked and walked to the beach. I took off my shoes and walked in the soft white sand. I could almost feel Dutch. Sure, the investigative plan was on the table, just like Dutch and I had written it so many years ago.

"Thanks, Dutch. We will get these guys this time! They fooled us once, but they can't fool us twice!"

If one assumed that the same scheme was being initiated here as in Asmara, then the same investigative plan would work just fine. Surveillance. I needed to take a look-see and discover what could be learned from the fuel deliveries. During the next few weeks I spent as much on-duty time and off-duty time as I could around the Department of Public Works. The fuel was delivered twice a week, Tuesday and Friday. Most deliveries were in the late morning. The company delivering the fuel was Long County Oil Company. Their yard and offices were just over the county line from us in Long County. I also noticed that the same driver always made the deliveries, a white male about 35 years of age. He always drove the same truck and trailer. So a step back in his schedule was in order. I did more surveillance on him and learned that he parked his truck each night in the company yard and drove his Honda to his small ranch home on the west side of Hayesville.

I then started following him on his runs on Tuesday and Friday. He was dirty! He would pick up his truck and trailer in the morning about 6:00 A.M., drive to the fuel terminal in Garden City and load his product. Then south on US 17 and just south of Midway he would turn down a small dirt road and into a barnyard. There he would pump fuel into a single-axle straight tank truck that looked like it could hold no more than 700 gallons. The truck was always backed in so I could not get the tag information and I also noted it had no commercial markings. Then the driver drove on to Public Works and made the city's fuel delivery. It was always Lucas signing for the delivery and walking back into his office with the paperwork.

I then initiated surveillance on the truck on the farm. Each evening after a delivery Lucas would return to the farm and drive the truck to a gas station near the I-95 exit. He would then pump the fuel into an underground tank. I was able to record the tag number of the truck. It came back registered to a different vehicle, a pickup truck owned by Lucas. What a tight wad! He was too cheap to pay for the commercial tag for the tank truck. I checked the ownership of the gasoline station and convenience store at the I-95 exit and found it co-owned by Watson and Falks. This case was a done deal.

I had taken about 10 rolls of film during the surveillances. That night I drove over to South Carolina to a shopping center and had them developed in a 1-hour photo shop. The next morning I was sitting outside the Chief's office when he came to work. I had the pictures and my logs, together with another copy of the Asmara case I had made.

I apologized to the Chief for not coming in sooner, but I did not want to look like an alarmist or be guilty of falsely accusing three rather senior employees. About ten minutes into my briefing he stopped me, picked up the telephone and called the Detective Commander and the Deputy Chief into his office. He then asked me to begin again. I went through everything I had to include the case from Asmara many years ago. All agreed that it was clear that there were irregularities. The unloading of the fuel on the farm was some type of theft for sure. And there was clearly reason to believe that the city was also at least a victim if not involved by the criminal actions of the three suspects.

I was not looking for a detective position or even another temporary assignment, so I made it clear I was delivering this for their use. Chief Rainer was a smart guy and read me immediately. "Joe, we are kind of tight in the Detective Division right now, but I think they can put a couple of guys on this. But if they get overloaded, we might call on you for some help."

I understood that was his way of keeping me on standby but also getting me back on patrol where he knew that was what I wanted.

# Chapter 18

## A Different Ending

I didn't give the case much more thought. I saw the three musketeers around town a couple of times so I figured the detectives were doing the paperwork drill, which as I had learned, can be a long haul. I pictured them up in their conference room with miles of paper spread out across the conference table, as they were late for dinner and missing the ballgames on the weekend. Then one day I got a message to see the Chief. I went to see him and he told me that the case had been made, that the District Attorney had signed off and the three suspects were going to be arrested in the morning. He asked if I wanted to be in on the arrest. I thought quickly and told him I was off the next two days and had a date tonight that might turn into a drive down to Jacksonville Beach. He laughed and said they had it covered and to have a good time. Good, I would be tickled to death to see these three arrested, but for some reason I just didn't want to get involved. I guess that if it couldn't be Dutch and me, then I didn't want to be involved.

I was off the next two days but I had no date. I went home, turned on the TV, and watched some baseball, then to bed. I could not sleep. I kept thinking about the killing of the Ethiopian driver and his wife. These three would be busted on theft, but not for the crimes in Africa. I lay in bed and thought about the case. I could not get to sleep. Then I wondered, would they try to knock this case off the tracks like the last one? Did our guys have any surveillance on the driver's house? It was 2:15 A.M. I got up, dressed in some dark clothing and got my 357 and a small J frame .38 for back-up and headed out. I drove to the driver's house and circled around for a few minutes. No surveillance. I could have quickly sniffed them out had they been in the area.

I drove about five blocks away and parked my car in the driveway of a vacant house. I scooped up several handfuls of dry leaves from around the yard and dotted them across my car. Good, it looked like it had been there a month. Then I slowly walked to the driver's house. I walked down an alley and hunkered down between two garages for 10 minutes. I was not being followed. I slowly continued to his house. It was a small ranch-type house. Windows across the front, two windows on one side and a back door and windows on the back, but no windows on the fourth side of the home. I took a lying-down position in the next-door yard under bushes on the side of that house that faced the window side of the ranch house. Good vision of the three sides that had access. I looked at my watch. It was 3:05 A.M. Wonder what time they had scheduled the arrests?

I had been in the bushes about an hour, wishing for a blanket and a cup of coffee when I saw a police car come slowly down the street. Was this the arrest team? It passed under a streetlight and I could not believe what I was seeing. There was Anthony Lucas driving a Hayesville police car. Sure, he had several at the city garage at any one time. The car went around the block twice, then killed its lights and parked down the street about three houses away. He sat in the car for about ten minutes. I guessed he was listening to the police radio trying to account for the on-duty officers.

He stepped out of the car, closed the door and turned his collar up to the cool breeze. He opened the back door and brought out a small frame rifle. He then slowly walked up the street in my direction. I pulled myself down into the dirt and felt like I was 10 inches under ground. Lucas turned up the sidewalk and walked right up on the front porch. I low-crawled out of the bushes and angled around so I could not be seen. I made it to the side of the house, and then slinked down the house to the edge of the front porch. The porch was about three feet above ground level. I was at the edge of the porch, right under the front door. Just then I heard the doorbell ringing and Lucas banging on the door. I got as low as I could and peeked around the corner. I then heard footsteps in the house and saw Lucas pull the rifle up and parallel to the ground pointed at the door. He was on the trigger. It was clear he would shoot when the door was opened. I pulled my 357 and held it at the ready.

Just as I heard the door being opened, I jumped up and screamed, "Police, drop it." He turned and was swinging it toward me. I fired three times and hit him each time.

Down went Lucas. The door opened and the man peeked out. I yelled at him, "I'm a policeman, call 911, report an officer involved in a shooting and order an ambulance. He looked at me but could not move. "Now, 911, ambulance!"

I knelt down next to Lucas. He was in bad shape. I had hit him three times and from my position lower than him, the rounds hit him in the stomach and drove up into his chest cavity. He was on his way out. I opened his shirt and he was gushing blood. It reminded me so much of Dutch that night at the PX Gas Station. The man's wife then came to the door and looked out. I ordered some towels. Just then I heard a siren and saw an unmarked Hayesville detective car skid up in front of the house. Detective Al Jenkinson ran up the steps. He was one of the men on the case. I gave him a thumbnail of what happened and he nodded his head.

Lucas then said, "I can't feel anything, I'm dying."

I told him that yes, he was bad and asked if he was Catholic. No, Baptist. I then asked him what he was doing here tonight. He said he didn't know.

"Listen, you are on your way to meet the maker, get it off your chest. All of it, starting in Africa."

Those must have been the right words. He started on the gas thefts going back to Asmara. He acknowledged working for Watson and doing all the dirty work on the thefts, to include the Asmara murders and tonight's attempt. As he talked I looked down at Al Jenkinson's hand. He had his small voice recorder to the side of Lucas' face. Lucas went on talking and stopped twice to say he was going to die.

He looked over to me and said his last words: "I'm sorry, tell my wife I love her." He was dead.

Jenkinson turned off his recorder and blew into it like the movies, like a guy blowing into the barrel of a gun. He smiled and said, "Best dying declaration I ever heard, and recorded, too!"

Watson and Falks pleaded out. Twenty to life for theft and murder, they owned the responsibility for the death of Lucas. The gas company driver got a suspended sentence in exchange for his testimony against Watson and Falks.

After sentencing I drove down the coast road to the beach and briefed Dutch. Just as I finished the wind picked up just a bit and blew hard against the wet rocks, making a very pronounced "Ohoooo" sound.

"Yes, Dutch, the case is cleared."

# Chapter 19

# I Could Not Believe My Eyes

I applied for a copy of the case with all enclosures and photos under the Georgia Open Records Law. I wanted to be able to freely pass the case on without a conflict of interest. Once I had it all I took a weeks vacation and drove up to the Eritrean Embassy in Washington, D.C. I met with the legal attaché and we discussed both cases for a couple of hours. I suggested that he apply for extradition for the two and have them tried in Asmara for the murder of the first driver and his wife.

I came back to Hayesville by way of Fort Gordon. I just wanted to see how things had changed. The MP School had moved to Fort McClellan, Alabama, and Fort Gordon was now overrun with signal school trainees. All of my old amigos had either shipped overseas or moved to Fort McClellan with the school. I got my coffee and got the heck out of there.

I got back home and went to work. Then about two months later, I got a call to go to the District Attorney's Office. I met with the DA, Mr. Tom Celadon, who said he had a request for extradition for Watson and Falks. It had been approved all the way from the State Department through the Governor and locally. Those two were going to Africa. Also in the packet was a subpoena for me to testify in Asmara at their trial. I would offer testimony on the original case as well as Lucas' dying declaration.

I thought to myself, "That was great, just great". I would be glad to see action on those two and I would be able to find out what had happened to Giorgina. Travel was less than a week away. The DA said I would remain on the city payroll for the duration of the trip, unless I elected to take some personal time along the way.

The Chief was good enough to authorize a patrol car to drive me to the airport. I was ready for this trip and had them take me to the Savannah Airport a good three hours early.

The route was from Savannah to Atlanta, to JFK, New York, to Rome and then the new Eritrean Airlines to Asmara. An Asmara police detective who spoke a little English met me at the airport. He immediately cautioned me on not being out alone in the city as it was very dangerous. War still lingered on and people still had a lot of hate left. He said Americans were often on the list of hated people because there was a lot of thought America had abandoned the country to be consumed by Ethiopia. He drove me to my hotel and said to stay and eat in the hotel and he would be back in the morning to take me to the police station.

The Asmara Police had made me reservations at the Hamasien Hotel, which was right downtown. Giorgina and I had often eaten dinner there years before. The hotel had a major face-lift and full modernization. It was first class. I got checked into my room and looked out the window, remembering how many times Giorgina and I walked down this street. Just a few blocks away was our favorite restaurant. I so much wanted to go for a walk, but thought better of it. Tomorrow would be a good day to find out the situation. I slept well that night.

The next morning my police escort met me in the dining room and had coffee with me. He was a totally different person, much more respectful. He told me that yesterday he had not known how famous I was in Asmara. He explained that Police Chief Adonay Bereket had directed him to take special care of me. Yes, Adonay had been Eritrean and would have been in a great position to move up after the war. We drove to the police station and walked to Adonay's office. He hugged me hard and kissed both cheeks. I returned the custom. We talked for three hours until the lunch hour. He had never met Giorgina but did tell me that the war had been terrible. He would not go into details.

The trial for Watson and Falks would be tomorrow. It would be short, for they had made full confessions in the hope of avoiding the death sentence. But Adonay said murder is a death sentence in this country. We had lunch in one of the few remaining Italian restaurants. I spent the rest of the afternoon with the prosecutor going over the trial. Later in the day I stopped back to see Adonay and he said to keep a low profile tonight but after the trial, we would tour Asmara and Kagnew Station. My driver then took me back to the hotel.

The trial started at 7:30 A.M. in the morning. Watson and Falks had an Italian lawyer and there was a representative from the American embassy to observe the proceedings. The first witness was the prosecutor. He took his oath and gave his testimony, or in our system what would be the opening statement. Since the defendants spoke only English, there was a translator that translated as the trial went along. I was next. I summarized our actions in the original case, then in the case in America. The tape of Lucas' dying statement was introduced. I authenticated it and then it was played. Next the two defendants testified. Both outlined a full confession. I guess they had hope of something other than a death sentence. I knew better than that. I had seen a lot of trials in Asmara.

It was not 4:00 P.M. yet when the three-judge panel pronounced them guilty and sentenced them to death by hanging. The hanging was to take place within three days. That was the end of that case. No appeals. No special consideration for them as Americans. No nothing.

That night Adonay and I went to dinner at a very nice Eritrean government restaurant. We talked a little bit about the trial and he thanked me for my help, but we put it behind us quickly. Adonay said he had put a detective on the Giorgina matter and hoped to have something tomorrow. We set a meeting time for the morning to ride around Asmara and see the changes and war damages. He drove me to my hotel and again cautioned me on the gangs that run the streets at night.

True to his word Adonay met me in the hotel for breakfast in the morning. He was in civilian clothes, so I expected he would be a bit more laid back, and he was. We drove around Asmara. There was some war damage on the outskirts of the city, but almost all of the beautiful Italian buildings were undamaged. We arrived at the former Kagnew Station. When the Americans left, it was taken over as an Ethiopian installation. Since the war, the Eritrean Army had used the facility. We approached the gate and the driver said something to the gate guard and we were immediately allowed inside.

I first saw the Provost Marshal Office. It was unoccupied and had been severely damaged by a mortar or some type of bomb. We went next to the MP Station. The windows were boarded up and it was being used as a warehouse of some sort. I looked over the door and could see the outline of the military police crossed-pistols logo under a couple of coats of poor water paint.

The CID office appeared well-maintained. It looked even better than I remembered. We got out and walked through the gate. We could not go inside the building. It was now some type of communications facility and had limited access. Funny, that is what it had been before CID moved out of the MP Station and into that building. I walked around back and stopped at the patio. The cement was cracked and broken. I stood there for a while with my eyes closed remembering the Saturday shrimp boils put on by Mr. Barkus.

Then I looked to the back fence line. There was Dutch's little herb garden. I quickly walked over to look. There were basal plants growing among the weeds. I guess they had been reseeding themselves over the years. It brought tears to my eyes. I could see Dutch on his hands and knees working on his small garden. It was time to go.

We got back in the car and Adonay said, "I want to show you one other thing."

We drove down the hill, past the Fiat garage and continued down a familiar road. This was the way to Giorgina's house. We had been riding for a couple of hours and Adonay had not said what had been found out about Giorgina. And I had not asked him. I feared bad news and I guess I was putting it off as long as possible.

I sat up straight in my seat and asked Adonay what he had found out. He clenched his lips and I looked into his face. Was it a sad frown or some kind of smile? I could not read his face. Just then we pulled up and stopped in front of Giorgina's house. How many times had I been there? It looked just as I remembered it. No damage and well—maintained, very different than many of the other houses in the area.

I got out of the car, walked up to the gate and peered into the yard. My God, there was my Fiat. It looked great, clean and shinning in the morning sun. I could not believe my eyes. I turned to Adonay.

He was repeatedly pointing to the house as he walked back and got into the police car. He said, "You will be fine." The police car slowly drove away.

I felt like I was going to be sick. I walked up and just as I was about to knock on the door it opened. There was Giorgina. She looked beautiful. The years had not changed her. I studied her and could not believe my eyes; she was just as I had remembered. I looked at her left hand. No ring! What was wrong with the men around here?

She smiled and said, "Joe, you are always late." She held the door back and waived me into the house.

And they lived happily ever after!

# About The Author

Joe Gillam was stationed in Asmara in the mid 60's after assignments in Japan and Vietnam. He continued in the Army with follow on assignments at Ft Dix, NJ, Korea, Ft Indiantown Gap, PA, German, and Italy. Master Sergeant Gillam retired from the U.S. Army in 1984 after his last assignment, Ft Devens, MA. Joe's entire Army service was in the Military Police Corps. His assignments included patrol, investigations, physical security, combat service support and 18 months of attachment to the US Marshal Service as a Sky Marshal in the early 1970's.

After Army retirement Joe moved to Hinesville, GA and accepted a position with the Hinesville Police Department. Joe held varied assignments including patrol, traffic crash investigator, traffic sergeant, hostage negotiator and shift watch sergeant. Sergeant Gillam retired from the Hinesville Police Department in 2006.

Joe and his wife, Chong, continue to reside in Hinesville and make travel their number one hobby. They are constantly on the go and just might turn up in on your street at any time.

This is Joe's first book. Keep your eyes open for his next one. He is gathering his thoughts on another story.

CPSIA information can be obtained
at www.ICGtesting.com
Printed in the USA
JSHW021746091221
21110JS00001B/62